DAVE DAWSON
WITH
THE AIR CORPS

by

R. SIDNEY BOWEN

Author of:

"DAVE DAWSON AT DUNKIRK"
"DAVE DAWSON WITH THE R. A. F."
"DAVE DAWSON IN LIBYA"
"DAVE DAWSON ON CONVOY PATROL"
"DAVE DAWSON, FLIGHT LIEUTENANT"
"DAVE DAWSON AT SINGAPORE"
"DAVE DAWSON WITH THE PACIFIC FLEET"

THE SAALFIELD PUBLISHING COMPANY

AKRON, OHIO • NEW YORK

CONTENTS

CHAPTER ONE

Hangar Flying

FREDDY FARMER scooped up a handful of sand and let it trickle down between his fingers as he stared thoughtfully out at the broad expanse of the sky-blue Pacific Ocean. He and Dave Dawson had been granted seven days' leave from special duty with the U. S. Armed Forces, and they were spending it at Laguna Beach, just a few miles south of Los Angeles, in California. Only three days of swimming and taking it easy in the sun had passed into time history, but Freddy was beginning to get restless. With the whole world at war, somehow he just couldn't relax and enjoy a well earned and much deserved rest.

"Dave, know something?" he grunted presently. "I've got a feeling."

The dark-haired, well built youth sprawled face down on the sand beside him didn't make a sound. He didn't so much as move a single muscle. Freddy looked at him, made a face, and jabbed him in the ribs with a thumb.

"I said, I've got a feeling," he repeated.

Dave Dawson groaned, rolled over on his side, and gave his English born pal an exasperated glare.

"There I was winning the war all by myself, and ten of the most beautiful girls in the world waiting to hang medals on my manly chest!" he growled. "So now, what?"

"For the third time," Freddy Farmer said evenly, "I've got a feeling!"

"Well, have it for the fourth time, and see if I care!" Dawson snapped. "Wake a guy up from a beautiful dream just because you've got a feeling? Well, go buy some flea powder, or something!"

Freddy grinned and held his thumb up, ready to jab it to the ribs again.

"One thing I like about you, Dave," he said. "You're always cheerful and gay. Never a scowl or a sharp word. Going to stay awake, or must I give you this again?"

"Do, and you'll have a three mile swim!" Dave muttered, but sat up just the same. "Because that's how far out I'll heave you. But very well, my little man. What's bothering you today? Tell Papa, and then he'll go buy you a nice big lollypop, all coated with arsenic! Shoot!"

Freddy Farmer didn't reply at once. He

played with the sand some more, and took another look at the blue of the Pacific.

"Well, I don't think we'll be here very long,
Dave," he finally said slowly. "I have the feeling that something is brewing, and about to pop,
as you would say. Did you stop at the desk for
mail when we left the hotel this morning?"

"I did not!" Dawson replied quickly. "And
if you must know the truth, my bothersome
friend, I had a feeling that there was something
there I didn't want to see. So I sailed right on
by without giving the mail box a look. But it'll
be there when we go back this noon. So what, so
what, I always say."

"I wonder what kind of a job Colonel Welsh
has lined up for us next time," Freddy murmured. "He didn't drop any hint to you, did
he?"

Dave Dawson snorted and made gestures
with his two hands.

"Listen to the guy!" he grunted. "Did Colonel
Welsh drop any hints? My dear young man, for
your education, Colonel Welsh is chief of all
U. S. Intelligence Services—Army, Navy, and
Air Corps. Very few people know that, how-
ever. He—"

"Yes, yes, go on!" Freddy Farmer cut in sarcastically. "He is mostly known as a colonel of infantry, but that is just a cover for his real job. It was Colonel Welsh who arranged for us to be transferred out of the Royal Air Force to duty with the American forces. Our first job was with the Pacific Fleet, and—and although you did your best to get our necks broken, I did manage to save the day for us.* Right you are! So much for Colonel Welsh's personal history. What I want to know is, *did* he give you an inkling of what our next job would be?"

"As I was about to say," Dave said patiently, "Colonel Welsh is the kind of a man who wouldn't even let his own shadow know when he was going to take another step. So that means he told me absolutely nothing. Of course he did mention—but skip it. Let it slide."

"No, certainly not!" Freddy Farmer cried eagerly. "What did he mention? Go on, Dave! Tell me!"

"Well, he is a very understanding man," Dawson said gravely. "He knows the load I have to carry when you are around. So—well, he mentioned something about how if I'd like to leave you behind next time—why, it would be okay by him. He—Hey! Watch it! I've only got

* *"Dave Dawson with the Pacific Fleet."*

two arms! Don't break both of them, you wild man!"

The last was caused by Freddy Farmer dropping down on top of him, and for the next few minutes the sands of Laguna Beach were flying in all directions. Eventually Dave broke free and leaped to his feet.

"Just what I mean!" he panted. "A very dangerous guy to have around. Never can tell when he's going to go nuts. See you in the Pacific, Apple Cheeks!"

"Call me Apple Cheeks?" Freddy roared. "Why, I'll—"

Freddy didn't finish. By then Dave was a streak of sun-tanned lightning heading for the water. The English born ace sped after him, and for the next fifteen or twenty minutes they forgot the war cares of the world and were just a couple of red-blooded fellows having a swell time in the water. But when they came up onto the beach again and dropped down on the sand, a tiny cloud seemed to steal across the face of the warm sun and they unconsciously looked at each other, grave-eyed and grim.

It was Dave who finally broke the silence.

"If I live out this war," he said with a short laugh, "I'm going to set me up in the crystal ball gazing business. I should make a million the very first year. I get the strongest hunches sometimes."

"I think I'll go into partnership with you," Freddy Farmer grunted. "I'm getting your habit of getting blasted hunches, myself. Just now—I had one. I mean—well, that is—"

"That there *is* some kind of a message for us at the hotel?" Dave asked softly. "Well, that's just the way I feel, pal. And you know me and my hunches. You can bet on them!"

"Well, once in a while, yes," Freddy nodded. "And I fancy that this is one of those times. What say we go up and find out, Dave? I think I'd go a little balmy just sitting here wondering. Wouldn't you?"

"Check on that," Dave said with a nod and a sigh, and picked up his bathrobe. "Let's go. Know something, Freddy?"

"Several things," the English born youth replied. "What is it now?"

"A hope of mine," Dave told him. "A hope that there really is a message for us at the hotel. I mean—for us to go back to work. This is a swell place, and all that . . . But—well, it makes me feel kind of a heel to be taking it easy here when there are so many others fighting and dying all over the world. Don't get me wrong, Freddy. I'm not trying to act the old medal snatcher, I just—"

"I know exactly, Dave," Freddy Farmer interrupted quietly, and flung one arm across Dawson's shoulders. "When there's still so blasted much to be done, it sort of gets a chap not to be doing something about it. Yes, Dave, I hope, too, that there's a message waiting for us at the hotel. And if there isn't—"

Freddy let the rest slide and shrugged.

"Yes?" Dave prompted. "And if there isn't any message for us there?"

"Then I jolly well think I'll wire Colonel Welsh," Freddy said, "and request that I be returned to duty."

"Took the words right out of my mouth!" Dave cried. "That's just what I was going to suggest we do. Well, keep your fingers crossed, kid. There's the hotel bus waiting. It won't be long, now—one way or the other."

"And, please, Allah," Freddy Farmer murmured, "let it be the way we want it!"

CHAPTER TWO

Orders For Action

.HUNCHES OR NO hunches, when the two ace airmen entered the hotel lobby a bell hop came over to them on the double quick. There was a mile wide grin on his freckled face, and in his hand he held an official War Department envelope.

"Just off the wires not ten minutes ago, Lieutenants," he said. "I was going to hunt you up on the beach. Thought you might want it pronto."

"You thought right," Dave grinned, and swapped a quarter for the War Department wire.

He waited until the bellhop had gone on his way, and then feverishly tore open the envelope. Freddy Farmer looked over his shoulder. It was addressed to them both, and it read:

"Arriving Oakland Base, San Francisco, tonight at eight. Take plane or train but be sure to meet me. Important.
                                   Colonel Welsh"

Dave read the wire through twice, then smiled and sighed happily.

"Well, there you are, Freddy," he said. "Dreams do come true."

"I certainly hope so," the English born youth echoed. "But he doesn't say anything except for us to meet him."

"He doesn't have to!" Dave growled. "Holy smoke! He says it's important. That's good enough for me. Look, let's get dressed and packed and go to the L. A. Base. I'd like to borrow a ship and go up there by air, wouldn't you?"

"Quite!" Freddy replied instantly. "Almost a week, now, since I've been up. Yes, I could do very nicely with an odd spot of flying. But I wonder what he's got lined up for us—if anything?"

"Stop wondering," Dave chuckled, and headed for the elevators. "It doesn't get you any place. We'll know tonight—and then maybe you'll be sorry you did find out."

"Not if it's action, I won't!" Freddy said fervently. "I'll be the happiest chap in the world."

"Next to me," Dave said. "And I'm still keeping my fingers crossed."

It was just under two hours later when the two youths, wearing the uniforms of Naval Aviation Lieutenants, entered the Field Commandant's office at the Los Angeles Air Base and saluted smartly. This was not the first time they had been at the Base, nor the first time, either, that they had met the Commandant. He returned their salute, and then came forward to greet them warmly.

"Welcome, Lieutenants," he said as he shook hands. "But save your breath. I know why you're here. Got a wire from Washington not more than an hour ago. I'm to loan you a plane on request. Okay. There're three or four hundred out there. Take your pick. Or do you want one apiece?"

"No, a two seater, please, sir," Dave said, straight-faced. "Lieutenant Farmer, here, hasn't flown for a week. So I'd better take him along as passenger. Get him used to the air again."

The Commandant laughed as the red rushed into Freddy's face, but there was frank admiration in the eyes he focussed on the English youth.

"A two seater it will be then," he said. "But I'm well acquainted with Farmer's air record. A week's lay-off, or a year's lay-off, wouldn't hurt his piloting skill any. And of course, that goes for both of you. So stop trying to put me in the middle, Dawson. You're both tops in my book. And that's that. Well, I suppose you want to get going?"

"If we may, sir," Dave said. "We really have all kinds of time, but—well, it would sort of feel good to coast around for a spell. But I guess you know how we feel?"

"Don't I, though!" the Commandant exclaimed, and sighed heavily. "I don't often give advice, but here's a tip for you two lads. Don't ever let them promote you to the job of a Base Commandant. All desk work, and mighty little flying. Keep in the air, boys. Keep in it as long as you can. Believe me, I know what I'm talking about when I say that. Well, let's go out and get your plane warmed up. I've got a Vultee two seater out there that's a sweetheart. But I'll loan it to you chaps. Let's go."

The two youthful air aces murmured their thanks and followed the Commandant outside. But there was a warm tingling glow in their chests, and a pleased and happy light in their eyes. The L. A. Base Commandant could have praised them to the skies, but all his words would not have been half the compliment that was his offer to loan them a Vultee two seater that was "a sweetheart." That meant that the plane was the Commandant's own personal ship, when he could use it. And he was doing them high honor to offer it for their use.

Half an hour later they thanked the Base Commandant again and took off in the Vultee with Dave at the controls, and Freddy Farmer riding the rear gunner's pit. Dave took them up to eight or nine thousand, and then started tossing the ship around a little, just to get the feel of the air again. That off his chest, he twisted around in the seat and grinned at Freddy. The English youth shook his head, made a wry face, and held up both hands with the thumbs extended downward.

"Simply terrible!" he shouted above the sound of the Wright radial in the nose. "Go back and do it all over again. And you call yourself a pukka pilot? Rubbish! But I say, Dave, now that we're up here, and have lots of time on our hands, mind doing something?"

"Certainly, if it's not for you!" Dawson shot back at him. "What is it?"

Freddy raised a hand and pointed eastward.

"Let's go inland a bit and follow the mountains northward," he said. "They're very picturesque, and I'd like a good look at them. Mind?"

"Okay by me," Dave replied with a nod. "Always did like mountain flying. Fair enough, then. Hang on, little man. Here we go."

Banking the plane eastward, Dave headed for the long range of towering peaks, then turned northward when he was over them, and throttled slightly. For a good half hour they flew along about the peaks, not saying more than half a dozen words to each other. The wild rugged beauty of the scene below was something that made words seem empty and futile. It was a scene that moved the heart rather than the tongue.

Suddenly, though, Freddy Farmer leaned forward and rapped Dave sharply on the shoulder.

"Off there to the right, Dave!" he called out. "About a mile, and down in that valley shaped like an S. I think—Dave! That's a crashed plane down there, or I'm crazy. Look! Do you see it?"

Dave stared hard off his right wing and down at the valley indicated by Freddy Farmer's pointed finger. It was several seconds, though, before he spotted the crumpled wings of a wrecked plane, and the broken tail that was sticking straight up in the air. But for Freddy Farmer he could have flown over the spot a hundred times, and not sighted anything but the trees. But now that Farmer's eagle eyes had picked it out for him, the crashed plane was as clear as day to him. He took a quick glance back at Freddy, nodded vigorously, and impulsively hauled the throttle all the way back.

"Check!" he cried. "And from the wing color and markings, that looks like an Army Air Corps ship to me. My guess is that it's a Curtiss P-Forty. I'm going down for a better look— and a landing, if we can make it."

"Of course it may be an old crash," Freddy said as he kept his gaze fixed on the wreck. "And the pilot has been rescued. But good grief, in this wild country a chap could be lost for weeks."

"You're telling me?" Dave echoed. "That's why I'm going to make plenty sure before I try and sit down. We've got an important date in San Francisco tonight, you know."

Freddy Farmer nodded absently, and then both boys shut up and concentrated all of their attention on the crashed plane. Dave took the Vultee downward, held it steady against the ever changing wind currents in among the mountain, and eventually was no more than a couple of hundred feet over the wreck. It was then that Freddy Farmer's sharp eyes went to bat again.

"It isn't an old crash, Dave!" he cried. "And there is the pilot chap, on the ground close to that buckled left wing. See him? He's alive, but hurt. He can't get up. He's waving to us. Dave, think you can make it?"

Dawson didn't reply. He had already seen the injured pilot waving for help, and he was now stabbing the ground with his eyes for a suitable place in which to sit down. He finally picked a spot no more than a quarter of a mile away. It was small, and mighty narrow, but he was sure that he could make it. If he didn't? He didn't bother to answer that question. Right now there was an injured man down there on the ground who seemed to need help badly. And that was the important thing.

"This is it, Freddy!" he called out grimly. "That narrow strip dead ahead. I'm going to shoot for it. Be ready to stick out your hands and push the tree trunks away!"

"Never mind the funny remarks!" Farmer barked right back at him. "Just get us down in one piece. That's all you have to worry about."

"A mere detail!" Dave growled, but didn't bother to turn his head. "Just a mere detail. Consider it as good as done!"

Perhaps it was sixty seconds, or maybe it was sixty years before Dave felt the wheels touch, and was able to start braking the Vultee to a gentle stop. Only when the plane was motionless, and just the prop was ticking over, did he let the trapped air from his lungs. He did it with a long shrill whistle and wiped beads of cold sweat from his face.

"I think it's safe to look, Freddy," he said. "Is that the ground we're resting on? Boy, oh boy! I'm still not sure whether I should believe it or not."

"It's true enough," Freddy said, and gulped. "But how you ever made it, don't ever ask! Very top-hole, just the same, Dave. One of the best bits of flying I ever saw you do. And I mean that, old thing!"

Dave wiped some more sweat from his face and legged out and down onto the ground.

"Thanks, pal," he said. "But I did it by making believe it was you at the controls. Okay, let's—"

Dave didn't finish. At that moment came the

agonized cry of an injured man through the trees.

"Help! Help! Over this way! Can you hear me? Can you hear me? Over this way— hurry . . . !"

Dave and Freddy simply glanced at each other. Then they spun around as one man and went plunging blindly back through the heavy valley growth.

CHAPTER THREE

Fate Laughs Last

THEY CAME UPON the crashed plane unexpectedly. One moment a solid wall of trees and heavy undergrowth loomed up in front of their paths, and in the next they were bursting through into a small clearing, and there was the wrecked plane. A single flash glance told Dave that his original guess has been correct. The plane was an Air Corps P-Forty. But he wasted just that single glance on the plane. With Freddy Farmer right at his heels, he dashed around to the other side of the crash and dropped to his knees beside the sprawled figure of the injured pilot.

The man's cries for help had obviously taxed much of his remaining strength. He was in a dead faint, and his face was the color of old parchment, save where it was smeared with blood. As Dave looked down at him he felt his heart turn icy, and then it seemed to loop over in his chest. The pilot was hurt badly, very badly. His chest was horribly crushed, and the fact that he was stretched out on the ground seemed to indicate that crash impact had thrown his body clear. He couldn't possibly have crawled from the wreck in that condition. That he had summoned up enough strength to call out had been a miracle in itself.

"The poor blighter," Freddy Farmer said softly. "There isn't anything we can do for him. I wonder what happened? He's wearing his 'chute. Why didn't he bail out?"

Dave started to speak, but he checked himself as the injured man opened his eyes. There was pain and bitter misery in them. And something else, too. Something in their depths. Dave had seen that in the eyes of other men on the far flung battlefields of the world. And he recognized it now as the Shadow of Death.

"Oxygen tank. Something haywire. Smelled funny. Passed out like a light. Woke—up— here."

The words were spoken in a whisper, and both Dave and Freddy had to strain their ears to catch them. As the man made gurgling sounds in his throat, Dave shook his head.

"Don't try to talk, old man," he said gently. "Just try and relax. We'll do something for you. Just take it easy. We'll get you out of here and in a nice hospital in no time at all. Just relax and don't waste your strength."

Dave knew that he lied as he spoke the words, but the injured pilot's suffering justified all the lies in the world. But the pilot knew that he was lying. The corners of his mouth twitched in a faint grin, and he shook his head a little.

"It's okay—know this is it. I don't mind, but —I must be in Frisco tonight. Urgent. Must see Colonel Welsh—must see Colonel Welsh— must see—him . . ."

The man tried to go on talking, but the hand of death was close. He did mumble sounds, but they made no sense to either Dave or Freddy, though they both strained their ears to the utmost. A terrible dryness was in Dave's mouth, and his heart was hammering against his ribs. For a crazy instant he wanted to shake the injured man back to consciousness and find out, what about Colonel Welsh? But of course he didn't do anything like that. He simply squatted there on the ground with Freddy Farmer and stared helplessly at the dying man. Would he go, now, or would he revive again long enough to speak more? Much as he wanted to know what the injured pilot had to say, Dave could not but hope with all his heart that the man might be spared more pain and suffering, and be taken to his heavenly reward in peace.

However, the spark of life burned fiercely in the injured pilot. Once more he came back to consciousness, once more he looked up into Dave Dawson's face, and once more his lips moved and whispered words.

"Tell—Colonel Welsh—Seven-Eleven—I'm sure—oxygen! Passed—out. Tell—tell him—"

The whispering started to fail, and Dave put his ear close to the man's trembling lips.

"Yes, old fellow?" he pleaded. "Go on! What do you want us to tell Colonel Welsh? We're meeting him in Frisco tonight."

The dying man's eyes lighted up with a sort of wild joy.

"Thank God!" came the faint sound. "Tell him—southern—southern al—bar—cur—keys. Understand? Southern al — bar — cur — keys. Seven-Eleven — there . . . Strike — soon! Hurry—hurry—hur—"

The whispering sounds faded away. The injured pilot's eyes seemed to give off showers of sparks. He heaved himself up on one elbow, tried to speak again, but failed. A long soft sigh slid out from between his lips. Then he slumped back on the ground. His eyes fluttered closed. And he lay still. Dave started to speak again, but he checked himself. He know that this pilot would never again hear a human voice in this world. He was gone forever, leaving behind the jumbled up sounds of words that represented some secret now forever locked in his brain.

Dave and Freddy slowly got to their feet, stood silently at attention, and solemnly saluted the dead pilot on the ground. On impulse Dave took off his tunic and reverently placed it over the dead man's head and shoulders. Then he turned and looked at Freddy.

"Did you catch all that?" he asked. "Did it mean anything to you?"

The English born youth slowly shook his head.

"I heard it, yes," he said. "But I haven't the faintest idea what he was trying to tell us. There were four words. He spoke them twice, slowly. He desperately wanted us to tell them to Colonel Welsh. I got them as Al, and Bar, and Cur, and Keys. Perhaps that's some sort of a code that Colonel Welsh will understand."

"Yes, it probably is," Dave said with a frown. "And I guess that means he was one of Colonel Welsh's agents. Gosh! This makes me feel like a grave robber, but I guess I've got to do it. Give me a hand, Freddy. I think we'd better search his pockets, and deliver the contents to Colonel Welsh."

"Quite," Freddy murmured, and dropped to his knees again. "I hope the poor chap will understand, wherever he is. Did you get that first bit he spoke about, Dave? I think he was trying to explain that his oxygen tank had been sabotaged. Somebody tampered with it, and he passed out when he took a bit. Phew! He must have come down at least eighteen thousand before he hit. A miracle the ship didn't catch on fire. Blast war, I say! How I hate the whole rotten business!"

"You can say that again!" Dave muttered grimly. "Okay. You take the things as I hand them to you."

Some ten minutes later the two youths stared at a tiny pile of personal belongings on the ground. There was a handkerchief, with no initial, a pocket knife, a pack of cigarettes, and a clip of matches. But there was one other article that caused them to stare hard and frown in puzzled wonderment. It was a plain copper disc about the size of an American quarter. It was absolutely smooth, and contained not a single scratch or mark.

"A lucky piece, eh?" Freddy Farmer grunted

as he met Dave's eyes.

"Maybe," the Yank born flying ace said with a shrug. "But do you notice something kind of strange, Freddy? This poor lad hasn't got a cent of money on him. Not a thing, except this copper disc."

"And not a single bit of identification!" Freddy Farmer breathed.

"So it's certain that he was one of Colonel Welsh's agents," Dave said, and bounced the copper disc in his hand. "And my guess is that this will identify him to Colonel Welsh. Gosh! How I hate, now, to keep that date in Frisco tonight."

"Why?" Freddy wanted to know.

"Because we're going to have to deliver some tough luck news to Colonel Welsh," Dawson said quietly. "And, maybe—and maybe this will wash out his reasons for wanting to see us. I hope not. I hope that—"

Dave shrugged and let the rest hang in thin air. He got to his feet, and nodded at Freddy.

"Time we got going," he said. "We'll mark this spot on our maps so Frisco Base can send an ambulance plane back for him. If we got in and out, so can an ambulance plane pilot. Happy landings, old man. You can count on all the rest of us carrying on for you until those Axis rats are finished for keeps."

"Amen!" Freddy breathed softly, and dropped into step.

Not another word was spoken between them until Dave had skillfully lifted the Vultee clear of the small narrow strip of ground and was nosing up into the California sky. Then Freddy reached forward and tapped him on the shoulder.

"Tip-top bit of flying, as usual, Dave!" he called out. "But tell me something. You started to say you hoped something, but you didn't finish. What was it?"

Dave flew on a bit before he finally twisted around in the seat and looked back at Freddy.

"Just a wild hope, and probably a crazy one," he said. "But I sort of hope that Colonel Welsh will give us the job of picking up where that poor fellow left off. Somehow I'd like to try and finish whatever it is he's started."

"And that makes two of us who are hoping!" Freddy Farmer echoed back instantly.

CHAPTER FOUR

Dead End

IT WAS EXACTLY five minutes to eight o'clock in the evening, and Dave Dawson and Freddy Farmer were seated on the observation platform of the Administration Building at the San Francisco Air Base. In the tower above them the Control Officer was bringing in Air Corps planes, and sending them off, with clock-like regularity. For the last half hour they had enjoyed watching ships of all types and sizes come and go, but now that the time for Colonel Welsh's arrival was drawing near, an eerie tightness seemed to grip their bodies, and the huge minute hand on the tower clock seemed to stop dead and not budge a fraction of an inch.

"If I start screaming, don't let them lead me away to a padded cell," Dave broke the silence. "But this waiting is getting me down for a fare-thee-well."

"You're not alone in that!" Freddy echoed grimly. "I swear I've been watching that clock up there constantly for the last hour. It's stopped, I'm positive. But blast it, my own wrist

watch says exactly the same time. Phew, how I
wish he'd come!"

"I do, and I don't," Dave said. "There's a
chance, you know, that we may be all wet. Maybe what we have to report to the Colonel won't
mean a thing to him."

"But he mentioned the Colonel's name!"
Freddy protested.

"I know, and that seems to clinch it," Dawson
said with a shrug. "But this war is so absolutely
cockeyed it's sometime hard to believe anything,
even your own name."

"You're just getting jittery, Dave," Freddy
soothed. "Relax, old man. There's absolutely
nothing we can do but relax. We've reported
the crash to the Commandant here. And the
ambulance plane left long ago. So relax, old
thing. Get hold of yourself a bit."

"Like you are?" Dave said, and grinned. "If
you don't stop yanking on those fingers of your
left hand, pal, you're going to pull them right
off. And besides, you drive me bats when you
do it."

"Do I?" Freddy Farmer snapped at him.
"Then let's make a bargain. I'll leave the fingers
of my left hand alone, and you stop snapping
and unsnapping that blasted wrist watch of

yours, what?"

Dave stiffened and glanced down at his wrist watch dangling by the loosened metal strap. He snapped it shut for the last time, and looked at Freddy. They both laughed, and a good bit of the tension from waiting was eased off. Then they instinctively glaced up at the tower clock, and felt even better. The big hands pointed exactly to eight o'clock.

"Well, that passed the time, anyway," Dave murmured, and got up and walked over to the railing. "Now, if he hasn't force landed, or something!"

"What a cheerful chap to have for a pal!" Freddy growled as he joined Dawson. "Fact is, he's right on time. A penny to a crumpet that's him up there just starting to circle and come down."

Dave sighted along Freddy's pointed finger and his heart leaped. An executive cabin type of plane was sliding toward the near end of the central runway. It had no markings other than the new Air Corps insignia of a white star on a blue field, with the old red disc missing. But staring at it, Dave felt certain that Colonel Welsh was aboard.

The two youths watched it slide down to a

perfect landing, and then taxi directly over to the Base Commandant's office. That was all the proof they needed. When you taxied directly to the tarmac in front of the Base office, you were somebody important. If you weren't, you got the hide singed off you for not going to the arrival check-booth farther along the field. A moment or two after the plane had braked to a final stop, the cabin door opened and a tall, thin-faced man in the uniform of an infantry colonel stepped out and hurried into the office.

"You win a whole bag of your English crumpets, Freddy!" Dave cried. "That's him. Come on. I guess we'd better go down and let him know we're here."

"As though the Base Commandant won't tell him!" Freddy murmured. "Bit of a testy chap, wasn't he, telling us to come up here and wait? That we were waiting for a Colonel Welsh didn't seem to impress him a bit."

"Why should it?" Dave replied. "We both know that the Colonel doesn't advertise. Besides, if you were commandant of a Base this size you'd be testy, too!"

"I would not!" Freddy snorted. "I'd be way past that stage. I'd be completely balmy, and don't think I wouldn't!"

"Who says you haven't been, for years?" Dave cracked, and started down the observation platform stairs fast.

On the ground he waited for Freddy; then the two of them started over toward the Commandant's office. They had gone but halfway when Colonel Welsh came out of the office, saw them and hurried over. He smiled faintly, then gave Dave a sharp look.

"Too hot for a tunic, Dawson?" he asked. "That's not a very military appearance you make. What's this I hear about you reporting a plane crash? No, never mind. I don't want to talk here. Follow me."

Dave nodded, but grinned inwardly, and dropped into step with the senior officer. The same old Colonel Welsh! He talked like a machine gun, and did things even faster. No wonder he got results where others had failed. He was a ball of fire on legs.

As though the two youths were not with him and he were trying to catch a train, the Colonel walked quickly over to the motor park, selected an Air Corps Staff car, and climbed into it. He motioned Dave and Freddy in back, tossed a slip of paper at a guard who hurried over, and stamped on the starter button.

"Car requisition signed by your Commandant!" the Colonel barked at the guard, and shifted into gear.

Dave and Freddy had ridden with the Colonel before, so they were already braced, and were not thrown completely out of the car as it streaked forward. A little under thirty minutes later the Colonel braked to a stop in front of an office building in downtown San Francisco, and got out.

"Follow me, you fellows," he said, and hurried into the building.

The elevator let them off on the fourteenth floor. The Colonel led the way along the corridor and stopped in front of a door that was marked, "Civilian Defense, Third Division." He tried the door, found it locked, and seemed strangely surprised.

"So?" he muttered to himself, and fished out a bunch of keys. "Must be late. But he should have been here hours ago."

He stuck a key into the lock, twisted it, and pushed the door open.

"Inside, you two," he grunted. "Select a couple of chairs and sit down. Maybe a couple of messages waiting for me. No questions. I'll answer them all later."

Dave and Freddy stepped into a fair sized office that smelled of dust and dead air. It was as though the office hadn't been used in weeks. But it was all in a tidy condition. There were three desks, twice that number of chairs, an entire wall lined with filing cabinets, a two-way radio, a bank of half a dozen phones, and a lot of hanging maps of San Francisco and the West Coast areas. The two youths sat down and watched Colonel Welsh go straight to the biggest of the three desks. He picked up a small pile of mail, riffled through it, and then dropped the lot disgustedly on the desk.

"That's funny!" he muttered in a low voice. "Closed tighter than a drum. Nobody here. No messages. I don't get the picture at all. I don't—"

Colonel Welsh stopped short and stiffened. Dave and Freddy jerked up straight in their chairs, and all three swung quickly around and stared at the door of a closet at the rear end of the office. For a brief second or two no one dared breathe. They had all heard it: the soft thump of something against the inside of the door.

"Sit tight, you two!" Colonel Welsh suddenly said in a low voice. "I think I have an idea what that was. Sit tight, though, and be ready for action just in case."

Dave snapped his gaze back to the Colonel, and saw a small but deadly looking automatic appear in the senior officer's hands as though by magic. The Chief of all U. S. Intelligence Services went across the office with all the noise of a chicken feather brushing across a strip of velvet. He froze at the door, then grasped the key that was in the outside of the lock, twisted it, and jerked the door open. He had stepped back quickly, but he checked himself in mid-stride and flung out his free hand and caught the body that fell out the door opening like a fence post. It was a man wearing civilian clothes, but with Civilian Defense insignia on his sleeves. He was bound round and round by ropes, and there was a handkerchief gag jammed in his mouth.

"Strike me pink!" Freddy Farmer gasped, and came up out of his chair like a shot.

"Sweet tripe!" Dave echoed, and got up also. "This is like a murder mystery, or something."

"Never mind the comments!" Colonel Welsh snapped as he gently eased the bound man down onto the floor. "Hand me that knife on the desk, one of you. And you'll find a small bottle of brandy in the lower right door of the middle desk. Confound my luck. This makes a mess of things, I'm afraid!"

A hundred and one questions hovered on Dave's lips, but he had sense enough to keep them there. Explanations would come later—probably. But right now the idea was to act, not talk. He got the knife while Freddy fetched the bottle of brandy. Colonel Welsh prodded the gag from the bound man's mouth, then slashed the ropes and pulled them off. Then all three of them started rubbing the man's wrists and neck. He groaned slightly, and a moment later his eyes fluttered open. He looked up at Colonel Welsh, and seemed to recognize him, for the blood started coming back into his face.

"Don't talk yet, Rigby," Colonel Welsh said gently. "Take a sip of this, first. Just a sip. I don't want you choking to death on me."

The man smiled weakly and took a tiny sip of the brandy the Colonel held to his lips. The fiery liquid seemed to do wonders when it hit the bottom of his stomach. He panted a couple of times, gave his head a shake or two as though to clear away the cobwebs, and then started to hoist himself up on his feet.

"Getting okay by the minute, sir," he said. "If you'll just help me to one of those chairs.

The underpinnings are still a little rubbery."

Colonel Welsh helped him across the office to one of the chairs. Then he let the man take another sip of the brandy. The second sip doubled the work of the first. The man pressed his hands to his face for a moment, but when he took them away there was plenty of color in his cheeks, and a clear light replaced the dazed glaze that had been in his eyes. He started to speak, but checked himself and looked down at his wrist watch. A worried frown creased his brows as he looked up again at Colonel Welsh.

"A good three hours ago, sir," he said in a rueful tone. "I guess I must wear cotton stuffed in my ears. I didn't—"

The man called Rigby stopped short and shot hard quizzical glances at Dave and Freddy.

"It's all right," Colonel Welsh told him bluntly. "Two of my men. Now, what about three hours ago? What happened? Give me all the details."

As the senior officer spoke, he swept the entire office in one searching glance, then brought his eyes back to Rigby's face.

"I was sitting there, as usual," the man finally said, and jabbed a thumb at the center desk, "doing some Civilian Defense work, but wait-

ing for contacts from you. Got your word that
you would arrive this evening. Got your word,
also, that Copper was coming up from Albuquerque. Well—I heard the door open a while
later, but I thought it was some Air Raid
Warden, and didn't pay much attention until he
reached the desk. But—then it was too late. He
came to the desk like a shot of lightning, and
the building fell down on top of my head. I
guess—I guess, sir, you'd better dismiss me and
send me back to laying brick, or something."

The Colonel was silent a moment; then a soft,
sympathetic sadness seeped into his thin face.

"We all fail to touch second base every once
in a while, Rigby," he said quietly. "Of course,
it's a mark against you, but your past service
record can stand it. What about this man who
slugged you? Get a look at him?"

"Just a look, sir," Rigby said with a heavy
sigh. "Medium height, medium build, and I
think he was on the fair side a little. Ten million
like him, I'm afraid. It was only a flash look I
got. I—By George! Seven-Eleven, sir, do you
suppose?"

Colonel Welsh's face darkened with anger,
but he slowly shook his head.

"No, I think not," he said. "In fact, I'm sure
it wasn't. The pickings around here would be

too small for Seven-Eleven. Besides, I have good reason to believe that Seven-Eleven isn't even in the country."

"But why slug me?" Rigby said in a low voice as though to himself, and stared around. "Can't see that anything's been touched. Besides, there's not a thing here that would be of any use to anybody."

"My message in code?" Colonel Welsh asked evenly. "You had destroyed it?"

Rigby's face went pale as death. He clutched the sides of the chair seat for a moment, then shot out of it and over to the middle desk. When he turned around again his face was the color of chalk, and there was the blaze of a madman in his eyes.

"That's what he got," he said in a hushed voice. "I was just putting a match to your code note when he came in. I remember, now. That's why I didn't look up at once. I—I was trying to get the sheet burning."

"But you didn't," Colonel Welsh said in almost a groan. "Well, and so that's that. You better go drop in at a hospital, Rigby, and have them take a look at that lump on your head. Take a cab. I'll contact you later."

There was the hint of tears in Rigby's eyes, and in his voice.

"Perhaps I'd better go jump off the Golden Gate Bridge instead!" he said with an effort.

"Don't be a fool!" Colonel Welsh said not too unkindly, and went over to him. "It was just one of those things, old man. A mighty tough break, but it could just as well have happened to me, or to anybody in the Service. If you feel up to it, chase along to the hospital. I'll contact you later. Now, don't be a fool, Rigby. Don't really get me mad, will you?"

"No, sir," the other said as he walked toward the door. "But I don't see why you're not, now. Anyway—thanks, sir. I'll make it up some day, I hope and pray."

"I'm sure you will, Rigby," Colonel Welsh said, as he unlocked the door and let him out. "See you later."

The senior officer closed the door, locked it again, and walked slowly back to the middle desk. He dropped into the chair like a man who has aged twenty years in as many seconds. The gaze he fixed on Dave and Freddy was bleak, and laced with bitterness and misery.

"I wish I were a courageous man," he said heavily. "I wish I had the courage to go jump off the Golden Gate Bridge myself. It surely would remove a lot of woe from my life!"

CHAPTER FIVE

Seven-Eleven

DAVE AND FREDDY didn't say anything for a moment or two. They simply sat still and looked at the Colonel as their hearts bled in sympathy for his visible suffering. Then Dave slowly licked his lips, and put a faint sharp edge to his voice.

"That's one way out of it, sir," he said. "But it still wouldn't help Uncle Sam much. Uncle Sam, and the rest of the United Nations."

"Quite!" Freddy Farmer echoed evenly.

Colonel Welsh stiffened a little, and a hard brittle light leaped into his eyes. Then he suddenly relaxed, and one corner of his mouth went down in a faint grimace of self-reproach.

"I deserved that," he said. "And thanks, you two. Trust you two to snap a man back to his proper mood. Among ten million other things, you're certainly a pair of tonics. Too bad all of us can't have you around at the same time. Seriously, though, I am in the middle of a horrible mess, the worst one I've ever got tangled in. And the rotten part of it is that I was so close to ironing everything out as nice as can be."

The Colonel paused, brightened visibly and made a little waving gesture with one hand.

"But things are never as bad as they seem at first look," he said. "Almost any minute, now, one of my agents may arrive. And then we can all get down to brass tacks and slug this thing through to a satisfactory finish."

Dave and Freddy looked at each other. Freddy bit his lip and then nodded.

"Go ahead, Dave," he said quietly. "He should be told, of course."

"Told?" Colonel Welsh echoed sharply. "Told *what?* What *now?*"

"I don't think the man you expect, sir, will arrive," Dave said slowly. "That's why I haven't got my tunic. I left it spread over his face. He crashed in a P-Forty. Told us his oxygen tank had gone haywire. Thought somebody had fixed it. We spotted the crash on the way up here, in the mountains near El Prado. He—died shortly after we landed and got to him. Was his code name Copper? Did he carry this copper disc for secret identification, sir?"

As Dave ran out of breath momentarily, he took the copper disc from his pocket and handed it over. The Colonel took it as though it were a red hot coal. He dropped it on the desk top twice and had to pick it up. Suddenly he picked up the knife and dug the point into the surface of the copper and made a long scratch. Leaning way forward, Dave and Freddy saw that there was silver under the copper. The Colonel dropped the disc on the desk for the third time and looked as if he were going to collapse and come apart in chunks.

"Tell me everything," he said in a hollow voice. "Give me all the details, every single bit you can remember. Did he say anything? Did he give you any message? Anything that sounded like a code word?"

Dave didn't answer at once. He half closed his eyes and thought back to that scene in the mountain valley. Then slowly he related word for word everything that had taken place, and every word, or syllable of a word, that had been spoken. When he came to the end he half turned and looked at Freddy.

"Did I miss anything?" he asked. "Leave anything out?"

"Not a thing that I can recall," the English born youth said. "I'd swear that was all of it."

"Well, there you are, sir," Dave said, turning to Colonel Welsh again. "If there were any

code words, they must have been that Al, Bar,
Cur, and Keys that he spoke. Do they mean
anything to you?"

The Colonel plucked hard at his lower lip,
and stared hard and savagely at the top of the
desk. Finally he made noises in his throat, and
shook his head.

"Nothing," he grunted. "Those four words
don't mean anything to me. I—What's the
matter with you, Farmer?"

The last was because Freddy had suddenly sat
bolt upright and was staring at one of the wall
maps as though it were an ancient ghost come
out of the past. He started as the Colonel spoke
to him sharply. The blood rushed into his face,
and he frowned in embarrassed indecision.

"Well, out with it!" Colonel Welsh snapped.
"You've come up out of nowhere with good
ideas before. What's it now? What are you
thinking about?"

Freddy Farmer hesitated a moment longer,
and a look of sorrow and regret came into his
face.

"Perhaps it isn't a mystery, sir, those four
words that poor chap spoke," he said. "That
chap, Rigby, spoke about receiving your wire
about Copper coming up. The place he was

coming from, sir. I just happened to notice it there on the map."

"Albuquerque," Colonel Welsh said. "Well, what about it?"

"Well—well, he had trouble forming words," Freddy said. "Say those four words together."

"Eh?" Colonel Welsh echoed.

"Freddy's right!" Dave cried. "Al-bar-cur-keys! *Albuquerque!* It sounded to us like *bar,* instead of *ba.* And we got it *keys,* instead of *que,* pronounced key. He was trying to tell us where he'd come from, and— Yet, doggone it, I wonder?"

"Yes, Dawson?" the senior officer prompted, as Dave hesitated and fell silent. "You wonder what?"

"He repeated those four syllables several times," the Yank born air ace replied with a frown. "And he kept saying, 'Southern.' And he said. . . . 'Seven-Eleven — there . . . Strike soon.' Did he mean that this Seven-Eleven is south of Albuquerque? Or did he mean something that we haven't got yet? And—well, is it all right to ask you about this Seven-Eleven, sir?"

Colonel Welsh didn't reply for a couple of minutes. He seemed to go off into a thought trance. He stared at Dave and Freddy, and also right through them. He played with the gashed copper disc with his right hand, and continually clenched and unclenched his left fist.

"Yes, it's all right for you to ask," he finally said in a gloomy voice, "but there's blessed little I can tell you about him. At least, blessed little that's definite and concrete. Back in Washington my biggest Axis agent file happens to be on this Seven-Eleven. But if you want to know the truth, I have a hunch I could throw the whole confounded thing into the ash can, and I wouldn't lose a thing of real value. In a few words, Seven-Eleven is Mystery Man Number One. He is Mystery Man X. And for the past couple of months he has been the biggest and sharpest thorn in the side of U. S. Intelligence. And for all I know right now, this Seven-Eleven may be a dozen persons, and not just one."

Colonel Welsh paused for breath, and fell to playing with the gashed copper disc again.

"Seven-Eleven," he continued eventually, "is only the name we've tacked on him. If you play dice you know that seven and eleven are the two lucky numbers. So we call him Seven-Eleven because he seems to have double luck in every single thing he does. In my file I have a report that states he was born in Germany under the name of Karl Bletz. That he came to this country shortly after the last war, and became a naturalized citizen under the name of Paul Benz. The report goes on to state that he returned to Germany in 1933 and hooked up with Hitler's movement. He's been back here several times, but the last time he was here was in 1938. He went back for good then, and went out to South America to boost German trade there, but actually to do Gestapo work that would estrange the South American countries from the United States. He made out all right on that job, particularly in Argentina and Chile."

The senior officer paused again, shrugged, and then continued with his story.

"Since then he has been like a lighted fuse ready to touch off anything that would hurt England's cause, and ours. Cargos arriving from U. S. ports have mysteriously burned up on South American docks. And our ship owners have had to take the loss. Many England-bound ships leaving South America never arrived. In fact, they were never heard of again. And lately, many of our own ships have gone down, and crew members drowned, because of him. I even have a report that he was at Pearl Harbor on that back-stabbing day of December Seventh. We feel sure that certain mysterious munition plant explosions in the U. S. were planned and carried out by his sub-agents. He—"

Colonel Welsh stopped short, gestured slightly, and dragged down both corners of his mouth.

"I realize that all this may sound just a little on the fantastic side," he said. "How could we possibly tell that he had a hand in all these things? Well, simply the way police forces can tell that a certain known criminal had a hand in several robberies, or murders, or what have you. The man's mark. His trademark, you can call it. A definite little touch to each crime that tags it as having been committed by the same man. Well, we've run into that same thing with this unknown, Seven-Eleven, as we call him. A couple of things here and there that are identical with things discovered at other mysterious explosions, and so forth.

"In other words, there is one man behind most of the Nazi spy doings in the U. S., and Central and South America. He is the cleverest agent ever to come from Berlin, and the luckiest. But he is also the most deadly. Get in his way, and you're a dead man. I'm sure he'd slay his own mother if it would help him any. But this I *do* know! Twelve of my crack agents, stretching from the Canadian border to the bottom tip of the Argentine, have been after him for months trying to trip him up, and catch him."

Colonel Welsh cut off his words with a harsh sound, and there was the glitter of highly polished steel in his eyes.

"That man, Rigby, who just went out," he said between clenched teeth, "is the only one of the twelve alive today. Eleven trained Intelligence agents dead, and we are no nearer to getting our hands on this Seven-Eleven than we were weeks and weeks ago. It's enough to make me want to cut my own throat!"

The senior officer gave a savage nod of his head for emphasis, then rested his elbows on the edge of the desk, cupped his chin with his hands, and stared flint-eyed off into space.

Dave waited a few moments for him to speak again, but when the man remained silent he leaned forward a bit in his chair.

"You sent for Farmer and me, sir," he said gently. "Did the job you had in mind for us have any connection with—with this Seven-Eleven?"

The Colonel looked at him, and grunted.

"Yes, it did," he said. "The pilot you saw die was named Tracey. He was in charge of all our agents stationed in Central America, though he was working on the Seven-Eleven business alone. Officially he was assigned to the Ninety-Sixth Attack Squadron in the Canal Zone, but his unofficial job was to pick up any leads on this Seven-Eleven if he could, and follow them through."

"And did he, sir?" Freddy Farmer asked eagerly.

"Yes, and no," Colonel Welsh replied. "I mean by that that he ran across something pretty hot, I think. At least he sent word to me in code to arrange for his recall to the States for a short time. What he wanted, according to his code request, was leave of absence from his Squadron to follow up something. That was three weeks ago. Last night he sent word to me in Washington that he had flown out of Mexico into Texas, and up to Albuquerque. He asked me to meet him here, and to have two qualified Intelligence men present who were also pilots. I was unable to contact him direct, so I couldn't learn more. I sent word to Rigby to expect him, and to expect you two, and myself. And of course, I sent

you word to report at the Frisco Air Base. And
—well, as to what happened after that, you
know as much about it as I do."

"Something big in our hands, almost,"
breathed Freddy Farmer softly. "What rotten
luck!"

"That's putting it mildly!" Colonel Welsh
growled. "God knows what Tracey's death may
have cost us—cost the whole world!"

"Maybe," Dave murmured softly. "Maybe.
But I made a kind of promise to Tracey. More
of a hope, it was. A hope that Freddy and I
might have the chance to carry on where he left
off."

CHAPTER SIX

Battle Plans

A LONG SILENCE settled on the office after Dave's words had died away in the echo. The room was as quiet as a church, yet there seemed to be a sort of tingling vibration in the air. Dave felt it, and so did Freddy Farmer. And so did Colonel Welsh, from the intent and set look on his face. Presently he nervously cleared his throat and pressed his two palms flat on the desk.

"And we've *got* to carry on where Tracey left off!" he bit off, tight-lipped. "We owe that much to his gallant memory. We owe it to Uncle Sam. We owe it to ourselves. But—but there's nothing to get our hands on, nothing to get our teeth into. Tracey died without telling you two a thing that we can use, or work on. It's a cold trail, a dead end street!"

Dave Dawson leaned back his head, and stared unseeing at the office ceiling.

"Let's draw a few word pictures," he said more to himself than to the others. "Let's put it like this. While serving with the Ninety-Sixth Attack Squadron, Tracey came on something hot. He couldn't do anything about it because of his Squadron duties. His actions would look funny, and—his Intelligence identity wasn't known to his C.O., was it, sir?"

"No, it wasn't," the senior officer replied quickly. "It—Hold everything! Good Heavens, the death of Tracey must have done something to my mind. There is one of his under-agents in Ninety-Six, a young Second Lieutenant Marble. It was Tracey who got Marble into the service about a year ago. Tracey trained him, and worked with him on a few unimportant jobs. But I don't believe Marble was in on the Seven-Eleven business. That was strictly a confidential thing among handpicked agents, all of them picked by myself."

"Well, maybe it worked a little differently in this emergency," Dave murmured, and stared at the office ceiling again. "Let's see. After stumbling across something, Tracey requested you to see that he got a bit of recall-leave. He left this Marble in charge—or at least with some kind of instructions—and started north for the States. He got into Mexico. Maybe the trail led him that way, or maybe it worked out quicker that way. We may never know the reason. All we know is that he entered the States through

Texas, went on to Albuquerque, and— Just a minute! Colonel, there's an Air Corps Base at Albuquerque. Can you call them and find out *how* he arrived? I mean, was it in a Curtiss P-Forty such as we found? Or did he arrive in some other kind of plane? Can you get Albuquerque on the wire, and find out?"

"I can, and I will!" Colonel Welsh snapped, and scooped up one of the phones.

Just seven minutes later he hung up and looked at Dawson.

"He arrived in Albuquerque in a Vultee attack ship, alone," Colonel Welsh said. "It was one of Ninety-Six's planes. His papers were all in order for having landed on Mexican fields for gas. His ship wasn't armed, so technically he didn't fall under the internment law. Not that Mexico would have enforced it. The plane wasn't in such hot shape, however, so he borrowed a P-Forty from the Albuquerque Base. So much for that. Go on, Dawson. What are you leading up to?"

"I don't know," Dave replied. "Just sort of feeling around. Guessing at a lot of things just to hear how they sound. But here's one thing that strikes me odd. And it may have a reason. You say, Colonel, that he asked you to meet him here. Right?"

"Right," the senior officer grunted.

"And you also say," Dave went on, "that you could not contact him direct. Right?"

"Right again," Colonel Welsh said. "So what?"

"Well, why did he say to meet him *here?*" Dave asked softly. "Why not fly directly to Washington to report to his senior officer? That's not strictly military—to wire your superior to meet you some place three thousand miles away. So it was important. Important that he meet you *here*. Why? I don't know. Now the other item. Your not being able to contact him direct. Why? Probably because he wasn't around. Probably because *he discovered that there was somebody on his trail*. That somebody had found out from whoever visited Rigby today that Tracey was flying up from Albuquerque. So—well, measures were taken so that he would never arrive. Somebody at Albuquerque did something to Tracey's P-Forty oxygen tank so that actually he was gas poisoned and knocked cold when he took the first sip as he flew at altitude over the mountains. And—and, by the best of luck, Freddy's sharp eyes spotted his wrecked plane. Do those guesses sound a little reasonable to you, sir? To you, Freddy?"

"It could be a mighty close to the truth account of what actually did happen!" Colonel Welsh said softly to himself. "But it still doesn't get us anywhere. It still doesn't give us anything to jump on."

"I don't agree with you there, sir," Freddy Farmer spoke up quietly.

The senior Intelligence officer looked across the desk at him as though he were a long lost brother with a precious family secret.

"Well, thank Heavens, you don't!" he breathed. "Go ahead and tell me why you don't agree."

The English born flying ace took a couple of seconds out to think up the words he wanted to use.

"I believe I know what is in the back of Dawson's mind," he eventually said. "We *have* got something. It may prove to be nothing; to be absolutely worthless. But we don't know about that yet. I'm speaking of this Second Lieutenant Marble with the Ninety-Sixth Squadron down in the Canal Zone. Perhaps there is the chance that he can give us a lead on what Tracey was working on. Is there any way you can contact him, sir?"

"Why, certainly!" Colonel Welsh replied quickly. "I can—"

"Contact him, nothing!" Dave cut in harshly. "I mean, not unless it is a personal contact. But Freddy's only come up with half the stuff I had in mind. Right here in Frisco—right here in this room—we have a perfect lead."

Colonel Welsh sat up straight and quickly glared about the office as though he expected it to fill suddenly with people.

"Here in this room?" he demanded, fixing Dave with his steady eyes. "What in the world do you mean?"

"Not in the room, exactly," Dave said with a faint grin, "but the man who went out of the room. I mean, whoever it was that slugged Rigby and stole your decoded message to him. He's here. And it's a cinch he's been keeping an eye on this place. So who says he won't continue to keep an eye on it? You follow me, sir?"

"Not exactly," the senior officer grunted. "But you're right when you say he's been keeping an eye on this place. I could name on the fingers of one hand the men who know this is not strictly a Civilian Defense office for this section of the city. And they're all trustworthy. Yet somebody else found out, either Seven-

Eleven in person, or somebody in his pay. Anyway, that's the end of this place for Intelligence contact work. I've got to dig up a new spot now, one that I hope will be fool-proof. No, I mean spy proof, I guess."

Dave frowned and gave a little shake of his head.

"Naturally, you know best, sir," he said slowly, after a moment or two. "As the saying goes, it's not for the likes of me to tell you your business. But—well—I mean—"

The Yank born air ace floundered to a stop, and a faint flush stole into his face. Colonel Welsh stared at him for a moment, and then suddenly chuckled softly.

"I seem to remember a couple of times when you weren't so polite to your senior officer, Dawson," he said. "And *I* was the senior officer. I understand, but forget it, Dawson. All this is just between the three of us. So give it to me right from the shoulder. What's wrong with my closing up this place as far as Intelligence work is concerned?"

"Everything, Colonel," Dave told him bluntly. "Close up this place and open another, and you'll lose the only contact you have with the enemy agent, *or agents,* working in Frisco.

Of course you haven't what you'd call a real contact with him now. He's just a man Rigby saw for a split second before he got slammed on the head. But maybe we could make a real contact with him."

"What's your idea on how to do it?" the Chief of all U. S. Intelligence asked quietly. "And what would we gain by making a definite contact?"

Dave looked at him, and grinned faintly.

"Maybe this one is going to hurt, Colonel," he said. "What made him come here in the first place?"

The senior officer stiffened slightly, and looked puzzled.

"What's that?" he echoed. "Aren't you making it a little complicated, Dawson?"

"Perhaps I am," Dave said with a shrug. "Perhaps I am, because it's not very clear to me. Let's put it this way. The object of our unknown enemies was to put poor Tracey out of the way, wasn't it?"

"Yes, of course!" Colonel Welsh replied sharply. "So what?"

"So this," Dawson said evenly. "It was done. But it wasn't done from this end. At least, I'd bet my shirt on it. Tracey's death was caused by somebody *at Albuquerque!* So why did that slugger come to see Rigby?"

"To get my code message," Colonel Welsh said. "I think that fact's obvious."

Dave leaned forward and held the senior officer with his steady eyes.

"And what did your message say?" he demanded.

"I've already told you!" the other replied with a scowl. "I wired Rigby in code that Tracey was on his way here to meet me."

"I follow your line of reasoning, Dave!" Freddy Farmer broke in excitedly. "He simply found out something he already knew!"

"Bright lad!" Dawson beamed at him. "Go to the basket and pick yourself a nice red apple. You catch on quick, pal!"

"I do more than that, my little man!" the English youth shot back at him. "That chap's visit here had no connection at all with Tracey's death. Correct?"

"Now, wait a minute, you two!" Colonel Welsh shouted before Dave could speak. "I'm supposed to be the expert on riddles, but, by Heaven, you've got my brain tied up in knots. What in thunder are you talking about anyway?"

"Why, that lad's visit here, sir," Dave replied with an innocent grin. "Why he came here. This is just a wild guess, of course, but I think he came here *hoping* to find out *more* from your wire."

"Ah!" Colonel Welsh breathed as his face brightened. "I get it now, of course. Just another bit of proof that I must be slipping in my old age. Maybe I should resign from the Service. Anyway, I see what you mean. The rat in Albuquerque found out about Tracey's wire to me. He then contacted his rat co-worker here in Frisco and told him to keep a keener eye on this office, because I would undoubtedly be wiring instructions here. Which I did. But, thunderation! What else did he expect me to say in my wire to Rigby?"

"That's anybody's guess," Dave said with a frown. "But somehow it spells WORRY to me, in big letters."

"Quite!" Freddy Farmer echoed, and gave an emphatic nod of his head.

Colonel Welsh flushed and threw up his hands.

"Confound it, there you go again!" he bit off. "Worry? What the blue blazes has worry got to do with it?"

"Plenty!" Dave threw the word at him. "Worry that maybe you *did* make telephone or telegraph contact with Tracey before he left Albuquerque, and that he gave you a good idea of why he wanted to see you here. So maybe you wired certain instructions to Rigby. But you *didn't* wire any such instructions to Rigby. So our rat friend learned nothing. So he's still in the dark about your knowing anything of poor Tracey's secret. So he must still be worrying."

"I get it, I get it!" Colonel Welsh murmured softly.

"I spoke about maybe something hurting, awhile back," Dave said, and pointed a finger. "I meant that maybe your phones here are tapped. Maybe this place is full of leaks. Well, there's one way to find out, and maybe get some results."

Colonel Welsh just looked at him with raised eyebrows as Dave paused.

"So let's put out a bit of bait, and see what we catch," Dawson continued. "Phone some cooked up message back to your Washington office."

"Such as?" Colonel Welsh grunted.

Dave didn't reply at once. He sat frowning off into space and absently tapping a fingernail against his top front teeth. Suddenly he took his hand down and snapped his fingers, and flashed a grin at Freddy Farmer before he gave his attention to the Colonel.

"Got it, I think!" he breathed excitedly. "Wire your office, in code of course, that Tracey is dead, but *that his message got through!* And that you are sending two of your agents to Albuquerque to begin operations there!"

"What operations?" Colonel Welsh demanded.

Dave laughed and snapped his fingers again.

"That's just *it!*" he cried. "That's just what our rat friend will wonder—and wonder plenty. So he'll probably do something about it, and you can nail him. If nothing else, that will put an end to the Number One Man here in Frisco. And there's just the chance that we may also grab the lad—whoever he is—at the Albuquerque Base."

"Yes, that'll be something," Colonel Welsh said grimly. "That will be a lot, in fact. And your words aren't riddles to me now. The two agents who are supposed to be going to Albuquerque with information? They wouldn't be you two, by any chance, would they?"

"They'd be anybody else over our dead bodies!" Freddy Farmer spoke up. "Quite. And

I think that's rather a clever idea. It coming from Dawson, I'm no end surprised. He's been reading books, I fancy, when I haven't been looking."

"See that window, pal?" Dave said softly, and pointed.

"Certainly," Freddy replied. "Why?"

"It only happens to be fourteen floors above the street!" Dave said darkly. "And you're not wearing your parachute now. Just keep that little item in mind, sweetheart!"

"If I go, there'll be *two* of us!" the English youth snorted, and then grinned.

"Okay, okay!" Colonel Welsh growled, though there was a smile at the corners of his mouth. "Recess is over, children. Let's get back to serious things. And it is *mighty* serious. We know what happened to poor Tracey, and I wouldn't want—"

The senior officer hesitated and gestured with one hand.

"Neither would we, sir," Dave spoke up quietly. "But this isn't any pink tea. And Freddy and I have played plenty of long shot chances before. So there's no sense talking about the danger part. Now, here is my idea. We'll go to Albuquerque by air, of course. And don't worry! We'll keep low enough so that we won't have to sip oxygen at all. So that angle's out. And we'll also give the plane a darn good going over before a throttle is opened wide. On the way, we will keep our eyes open. And every minute after that."

"You could be attacked from the air," Colonel Welsh said with a scowl. "It's happened before. And this time it might be odds that you two sky scrappers couldn't match." *

"That's one of the chances we take," Freddy Farmer said gravely. "But I've got an idea. Why not have another plane follow us—one piloted by one of your agents, sir? Then if Dave and I bump into trouble, he can give us a hand. Then, too, he might spot the chap hiking after us, scare him off, and trail him back home. Then you'd have him, nice as can be. And in his secret drome hide-out, no doubt."

"Somebody else has been reading books on the sly, too!" Dave said with a chuckle. "Pick yourself another apple, Freddy. That was tops for an idea. Don't you think so, sir?"

"Well, it would make me feel a lot better to work it that way," the Chief of U. S. Intelligence said. "And of course, I'll arrange—and

* *"Dave Dawson with the Pacific Fleet."*

not from *this* office—for a couple of my men to keep an eye on you when you arrive in Albuquerque. Then if somebody gets on your tail down there my agents can close in and grab him. But—"

Colonel Welsh let the rest hang in mid air and sat chewing on his lower lip in brooding silence.

"So what?" Freddy Farmer said. Then catching himself and blushing slightly. "I mean, sir, what were you going to say?"

"Supposing we have all the luck in the world," the senior officer said, as though talking to himself. "Supposing we catch the Axis rat at this end, and at the Albuquerque end. What then? Notwithstanding what we read in the papers lately, I don't think we'll be able to learn a lot from our two prisoners. Most certainly, nothing that would make it possible either to get our hands on this confounded Seven-Eleven, or to learn the secret poor Tracey was never able to reveal. And that, of course, is our real goal. That is, if it's possible to have a goal in this mess."

"Well, we've just been talking about this end of things, sir," Dave said. "Just a way to clear up a couple of puzzling details. When Freddy and I reach Albuquerque, we certainly don't intend to stop there."

"What's that again?" Colonel Welsh asked sharply.

"Quite!" Freddy Farmer echoed. "I don't get the point of that one, myself."

Dave turned to him, and grinned.

"Ever see the Panama Canal, Freddy?" he asked.

"Eh?" the English youth ejaculated as his eyes flew open wide. "Why, no, never. But I've always heard it's quite a wonderful sight to see."

"It's more than that," Dave said firmly. "You'll get a big kick out of seeing it, particularly from the air. You see the whole works that way, from end to end. Oh, sure—"

"Just a minute, now!" Colonel Welsh cut in. "Why should you and Farmer go to the Canal Zone? What in thunder do you—?"

The senior officer stopped short, clenched his teeth in a gesture of self-exasperation, and whistled air between them.

"Of course, of course!" he grated. "What in thunder is the matter with me today."

"You get the idea, sir," Dave said with a grin. "Second Lieutenant Marble, of the Ninety-

Sixth Attack Squadron, is in the Canal Zone. Can you arrange with Army Air Corps H. Q. in Washington to have us assigned for duty with the Ninety-Sixth?"

"I can do much better than that," Colonel Welsh replied. "If you were assigned strictly to the Squadron for active duty, your chances of getting around—in the event you did get hold of something—might be a bit limited. And that's not even mentioning the suspicions you might create. I'll see that you are assigned to Ninety-Six, but for special duty, we'll say. It will appear that you're making some kind of an inspection trip on orders from Washington. That way you can come and go as you please, and nobody will think anything of it."

"Swell!" Dave breathed. "It couldn't be better."

"If, and when, you arrive in the Canal Zone," Colonel Welsh said almost in a tone of prayer.

"Oh, we jolly well will, sir!" Freddy Farmer spoke up. "Now that I've the chance to see that wonderful feat of engineering, no blasted Axis agents are going to stop me. At least, not if I can help it!"

"Atta boy, Freddy," Dave chuckled. "We'll give them the works, hey, kid? Well, Colonel,

I guess that's about all, isn't it? Isn't now as good a time as any to make that Washington call, and bait our little trap?"

The Chief of all U. S. Intelligence Services drummed his fingers on the desk for a moment, and then nodded.

"Yes, I guess it is," he grunted. "And I hope you're right, Dawson. I hope our friend did put a smooth one over on me, and that he tapped into these things."

And on saying that, the Colonel reached out a hand and pulled one of the phones to him.

CHAPTER SEVEN

Missing Wings

IT WAS EARLY the next morning and the first flaming rays of the new day's sun were just shooting up over the peaks of the mountains to the east. The last of the thin night fog was drifting out across San Francisco Bay, leaving the air washed and crisp and tangy. Though it was still early, activity at the Frisco Air Corps Base was in full swing. Swarms of wings flashed back and forth across the robin's-egg blue sky, and the air was filled with the thunder and power whines of many engines.

Down on the field, Dave and Freddy stood beside the Vultee they had flown up in from Los Angeles. Colonel Welsh was with them, and although the pilots' faces were bright with eager expectation of new adventures before them, there was no eagerness in the Colonel's face. There wasn't even so much as the ghost of a smile. His eyes were somber and brooding, and there was a tightness about the corners of his mouth. Dave glanced at him, and grinned.

"Chin up, white tie, and all that sort of thing,

as Freddy would say, sir," he said. "This will probably turn out to be nothing more than a swell joy ride. Who knows? Maybe my ideas on the wire tapping were as wet as the Bay over there. Please don't feel so tough about it, Colonel."

The senior officer forced a smile to his lips, made a little gesture with his hands, and sighed.

"I know, I know," he said. "I always act like an undertaker whenever I see any of my agents off on a mission. Can't seem to change, or get used to it. I guess it's because it gets me inside that I'm not going along, that I've got to stick here and take care of all the confounded paper work. Makes me feel useless, like a doddering old man too old to take part in the tough jobs."

"Oh, I say, hardly, sir!" Freddy Farmer said with a laugh. "If there weren't the brains for the paper work, as you call it, there wouldn't be any jobs for the agents to tackle. And I fancy, sir, there was a time not so long ago when you were the one who was being seen off by some other senior officer."

"Yes, you're right, Farmer," Colonel Welsh nodded sadly. "There was a day like that. But it seems centuries ago. I swear, if I had it all to live over again I'd never let them push me up to a post of important command. When you're on the way up you never stop to think how lucky you are you haven't reached the top yet. But I suppose that comes under the heading of ambition, or something."

"That makes two," Dave chuckled. "Only yesterday the Base Commandant at L. A. was telling Freddy and me the same thing. And by the way, sir, is that why you made us a couple of captains in the Air Corps, instead of colonels or generals?"

Colonel Welsh laughed out loud and shook his head.

"No, not for that reason," he said. "True, despite your youthful looks, you might get by as colonels. But not generals. We don't make them that young, yet. No. As captains you can mingle with the higher ranks if you have to, and not appear as though you were reaching for the moon. And as captains you can mingle with the lower ranks, and enlisted men, and not appear as though you were out sticking your noses into things. Matter of fact, I've always regarded a captaincy as the halfway mark in a man's military career. As a captain he still has close contact with those on the bottom of the ladder, and new contacts with those on the top. But—here

I stand gabbing, and you two are just busting to get away. Right?"

"Well, it has to happen sometime, sir," Dave said kindly. "And—well, count on us to stay in there pitching to the very end, regardless of what the end may be."

"Here, drop that sort of talk!" Freddy Farmer cried scornfully. "You'll have me flooding that rear cockpit with tears. One thing, sir. You'll be sure to make it all right with the Base Commandant at Los Angeles? I mean, about our taking his plane? After that bit of luck yesterday—well, the ship is sort of a good fortune charm, if you understand what I mean."

"Perfectly," Colonel Welsh said gravely. "And don't worry about the L. A. Base Commandant. He happens to be one of the whitest men in the Air Corps. Besides, when he loaned you his ship in the first place, that meant it was yours as long as you wanted it. He's that way. Now—well, get out of here before I change my mind! I feel like the executioner at Sing Sing waiting to throw the switch. Get off with you. Good luck. . . . And may He watch over you as He has in the past."

"Thanks, sir," Dave said with an effort. "And —so long."

"Quite, sir," Freddy Farmer murmured. "Happy landings until we meet again—which of course will be very soon."

The two flying aces clicked their heels, saluted smartly, then turned abruptly away and climbed into the Vultee's pits. Dave ran his eye over the instruments in an automatic check, opened his throttle a bit to "blow" his engine and clear the cylinders of dead gas fumes. Then he opened it all the way and sent the Vultee streaking straight out along the cross-field runway. He had it off and in the air in no time, climbing smoothly up toward the dawn sun-flooded heavens.

At five thousand he leveled off, circled the field a couple of times in an air salute to Colonel Welsh down on the ground, then dipped his wings and cut around to a crow flight course across the mountains and southeastward to Albuquerque, New Mexico. Not until San Francisco was out of sight behind the tail did he turn around and grin at Freddy.

"Gee, I'm sorry, Freddy," he said above the roar of the engine in the nose. "I didn't even give it a thought. But it's not too late yet. If you want to, it'll be perfectly okay by me pal."

The English born youth looked surprised,

and then slowly suspicion crawled into his eyes.

"What would be perfectly okay by you?" he demanded. "What didn't you think of this time?"

"Why, you, of course!" Dave replied as though Freddy should know it. "I didn't once ask if you'd rather not come along with me. I— I guess I just sort of took it for granted. But I can still skip back, and land, and dump you off, you know."

No anger showed in Freddy Farmer's face. He just looked at Dawson in sad sympathy, and sighed heavily.

"Listen to the bloke, will you?" he groaned. "Of all the cheeky ideas he gets. Didn't ask *me* if *I'd* rather not come! Well, I like that. When the truth is that Colonel Welsh said to me, out of your hearing, he said—'I say, Farmer, if you don't think Dawson would be of any value to you this time—!'"

The English youth cut off the rest and made a little significant gesture. Dave glared daggers at him, and then chuckled.

"Chalk one up for you, pal!" he cried. "I walked into that one with my eyes wide open, and got clipped. Okay. Kidding is off the books from here on in. Have you seen any sign of that agent who is supposed to tag along after us—just in case? He's flying a Navy Grumman job with Air Corps markings. I saw his ship over on the other side of the field."

"So did I," Freddy replied. "But I haven't seen him since. And I've been looking. Perhaps he decided not to get close enough for us to see him. Then the other bloke wouldn't see him either. I say, Dave, do you really think that baited trap idea will work?"

"I don't know," Dawson replied with a scowl. "Right now the hunch department isn't working. But I hope he does show up. When I think of poor Tracey—"

Dave lifted a hand and slowly closed it into a rock hard fist to indicate the rest of his sentence.

"Quite!" Freddy Farmer echoed, and patted the butts of his rear cockpit guns. "And right now I'm not sure I'd hold my fire if the blighter jumped out with his parachute. But it's the dirty rotter at the Albuquerque end I'd rather meet. He's the beggar who really did in poor Tracey."

"Well, let's hope this is our lucky day," Dave said. "Let's hope we get a good fair crack at both of them, or the six, or the dozen of them, if there are that many!"

With a nod for emphasis, Dave turned front and stared flint-eyed at the banks of clouds that were beginning to pile up above the eastern slopes of the mountain range. After a while the flinty look died out of his eyes, and was replaced by a look of thoughtful speculation. Then suddenly he grinned to himself.

"Guess this is the way with war," he murmured softly, "at least with Intelligence work. You get faced with a mystery that hasn't any strings hanging out of it at all. So you grab at what you *hope* is a string, and follow it through. If you're lucky, one thing leads to another, and you begin to get results. If you're not lucky, you get kicked in the face, and most times end up in a hole six feet deep. So here's hoping Lady Luck is still smiling on Freddy and me!"

"What's that you said, Dave?" came Freddy Farmer's voice. "Or is it just this morning sun that makes you mumble in your beard?"

"I haven't a beard," Dave slapped back at him. "And besides, I don't mumble. I was just telling myself that Intelligence work is all pretty much alike. I mean, you start with nothing, and hope you'll end up with all the correct answers."

"Absolutely right," the English youth agreed readily. "And I fancy the insane asylums are full of chaps who took up Intelligence work. I say! Aren't those mountains beautiful? You certainly do have wonderful scenery over here in America. No wonder you fought so hard in the Revolutionary War."

It was too perfect an opening for Dave to pass up. He twisted around in the seat and grinned broadly at his closest pal.

"Fought hard?" he echoed scornfully. "Nuts. It was a cinch. Why, I've read in history books where the American soldiers only used their right hands. Kept the left ones tied behind their backs."

Freddy Farmer made a face and stuck his nose in the air in a sniffing gesture. But as soon as he did that he stiffened slightly, narrowed his eyes and peered hard off to the right.

"Look at that plane over there, Dave!" he cried, and pointed. "It's one of your light plane affairs, one of your two-cylinder Grasshopper ships, as you call them. The chap's crazy to fly that thing around these mountains. Wind currents can bash him against a slope in no time. However, you Yanks!"

Dave didn't comment on the last. He had picked out the small plane silhouetted against the towering banks of clouds. It was one of those puddle-jumping Taylor Cubs, and it was dangerously close to the wind and squall-swept mountain sides. He could see it hit air current after air current and bounce about in the rough air like a cork in a heavy sea. The plane reminded him of a swimmer going against the tide. The plane was staggering forward, staggering toward a point that would take it across the Vultee's path of flight.

"Maybe he's some guy who got disappointed in love," Dave ventured the guess aloud. "Or maybe he just doesn't give a darn. But he seems to be getting clear of the mountains okay. So we should worry. I guess he must have slipped through from the other side. What was that crack about us Yanks?"

"I don't remember," Freddy grunted absently. "I wonder about that chap over there, though. What do you suppose he could be doing in among those jagged sloped mountains?"

"I wouldn't know," Dave replied with a chuckle. "But being as how you're such a curious cuss, I'll ask him when he comes in."

"Eh?" Freddy echoed.

"Skip it, pal!" Dave laughed. "I was only— Hey! The guy's in clear air, now, and he's making a beeline for us. And from here it looks like he's half standing up and waving at us out the side window."

"That's right!" Freddy cried, squinting across the mile or so of air space that separated the two planes. "The blighter is waving his arm off for fair. Now what, I wonder?"

"Search me," Dave said. "But keep your eyes skinned, Freddy. This may be the beginning of some funny business. It's up to us to be cagey of even a guy on a bicycle."

"Have no fear of that!" the English youth said grimly. "But I imagine he's pretty harmless. Can't say that I see his dinky little air kite bristling with machine guns."

"But you can't see into the cabin!" Dave barked. "So don't go taking things on face value. Be ready to grab hold of your hat in case he starts pulling something out of the air."

Dave wasn't sure whether Freddy snorted or not. Besides, he was too busy watching the small light plane draw closer and closer. A very familiar tingling sensation had come to the back of his neck. It made him a little annoyed to experience the sensation, because it undoubtedly was crazy to think that that little winged sky kite could give the well gunned Vultee any trouble. Still, the feeling was there at the back of the neck, and too many times in the past had it served as the advance warning of trouble for him completely to ignore it. And so he watched the small plane wing in close, but he sat stiff and taut in the seat, and every nerve and muscle was tensed for instantaneous, lightning fast action.

When it got in real close he could see that only the pilot was in the small cabin. There was no passenger in the other seat. For a second his heart looped over, and he got set to bank the Vultee off, when the smaller plane continued to head dead for him. However, in the last moment allowed the light plane swung around until it was flying wing tip to wing tip with the Air Corps ship. Dave automatically eased back the throttle to let the other keep pace, and stared across the air space at the light-complexioned, flaxen-haired man in the Cub's cabin.

At that moment the Cub's pilot put his hand out the cabin window, made frantic motions with it and pointed eastward and down.

"He seems to want us to go down, Dave!" Freddy said.

"He's got another think coming!" Dawson grunted back, and shook his head.

Then on sudden thought he motioned to the Cub pilot to cut his throttle completely, and at the same time eased the Vultee's Cyclone down to a murmur. Then he shoved back his glass hatch and cupped a hand to his lips.

"What's the matter?" he roared at the top of his voice.

Both planes were nosing down into a flat glide, but the Vultee was slowly drawing ahead of the butterfly type of plane. The pilot's voice came to Dawson's ears as a distant echo.

"Trouble—other side of mountains. Need— help—bad! A crack-up! Need help—bad! My —plane—too—small!"

Dave thought the other pilot shouted something more, but he couldn't tell for sure because the Vultee had pulled down way ahead of the smaller craft. Still keeping the engine idling, Dave pulled up the nose and hovered close to the stalling point while the Cub pilot used his engine and came up alongside again.

This time the light plane's pilot almost fell through the cabin window, so wild and frantic were his signals to Dave. And his voice rose as high as the scream of a woman.

"Crash! Crash! People hurt! Need help! Need help! Other side of range! Follow me down. Need help bad!"

"What shall we do, Dave?" came Freddy

Farmer's voice close behind Dawson. "Think the chap really means it? Or is this some kind of a funny game? He certainly looks excited enough. What do you think?"

Dave just shrugged and didn't answer for a moment. He stared hard across the mountain peaks as though that would permit him to see what was on the other side. He saw nothing but tree-covered slopes, and jagged rocks, and deep ravines, of course. On impulse he twisted around in the seat and looked back in the general direction of San Francisco. There was nothing there but blue sky and blooming patches of pure white clouds.

"Wonder how far back Colonel Welsh's agent is?" he spoke the question aloud. "By rights he should be near enough to see this light plane lad, and get curious and close in for a better look."

"That's what I've been wondering, too!" Freddy called out. "Strikes me as a bit strange we haven't seen hide nor hair of him since we left. Maybe he didn't get off."

Freddy Farmer's last words caused Dave to stiffen slightly, and a tingling ripple passed through his body. He looked at the English youth and half closed one eye.

"Maybe you've got something there, pal," he muttered. "Maybe our escort *didn't* get off Frisco Air Base. But if this lad's not kidding, and there is a crash with injured people over there beyond the mountains—"

Dave let the rest trail off and scowled at the banks of clouds. If there was a crash and injured people in need of help, he wanted to lend that help even though he and Freddy were on an important military mission. After all, injured people— Yct, confound it, there seemed to be something inside of him that wouldn't agree. A tiny voice kept yelling for him to ignore this pleading pilot and fly on to Albuquerque.

"Perhaps a look wouldn't hurt any, Dave," Freddy spoke up. "We could take a look, and if there is a crash send a radio to the nearest air field. What do you say to that?"

Dave didn't say anything to that. In fact, he hardly heard what Freddy Farmer was saying. At that moment he had suddenly spotted two dots high up in the banked clouds to the east, two moving dots that were hugging the shadows cast by the lumpy clouds. And he didn't need anyone to tell him that they *weren't* just a couple of soaring eagles!

CHAPTER EIGHT

Screaming Death

FOR PERHAPS TEN full seconds Dave stared brittle-eyed at those two moving dots. Then he took his eyes off them and looked at the Cub cabin monoplane. The little craft was doing its best to keep pace with the Air Corps plane, and its pilot was still waving his arm out the window and trying to make his screamed words of pleading carry across the air space that separated the two planes. As Dave looked at him he suddenly realized that he had been automatically swerving the Vultee to the left. This was because the Cub pilot kept swerving in a little too close for comfort, and Dave wasn't taking any chances of a mid air tangle of wings.

But now that he had seen those two moving dots, the Cub pilot's maneuvering meant something entirely different. Without appearing to do so, the Cub pilot was forcing the Vultee eastward and toward a point directly under those two moving dots high in the air. Dave grinned faintly, but a steel hard look crept into his eyes. He suddenly turned his head toward the Cub pilot and nodded it violently. Then he cupped both hands to his mouth.

"Okay!" he roared. "Get out in front and lead the way!"

The Cub pilot stopped waving instantly, and his face beamed with gratitude. He gave his small engine all the power it could take and pulled out in front of the well throttled Vultee.

"I guess this is best, Dave!" Freddy said. "Might as well take a look, just in case, what?"

Dave waited until the Cub light plane was a good bit in front and bearing around to the east. Then he looked back at Freddy and winked.

"One up on you this time, sweetheart," he said. "The old Farmer eagle eye missed the pitch this time. I think we're in for a bit of action. Anyway, I kind of hope so. Take a gander up and to the east, Freddy. That darker bank of clouds. See what I mean? And they're not a couple of sparrows, either. Can you make out the types?"

The English youth blinked, looked puzzled for a brief instant, then lifted his eyes and fixed them on the cloud bank. Dave, watching him, saw amazement and then anger flood Freddy's face. When Farmer lowered his gaze his eyes were startlingly cold and hard.

"The dirty blighters, if that's what they're up to!" he bit off. "Get us started on a supposed mercy errand, and then try to drop down on our necks."

"Try, is right!" Dave chuckled. "But we've seen them first. Okay, Freddy! There're only two of them. Get set to teach somebody a little lesson he won't be forgetting for a long time. We'll let them come down close, but not too close. Look! They're banking around and starting down. Well, knock me for a loop! A couple of Waco biplane speed jobs! Think we should go through with it, Freddy? Or should we pull out and tend to our own knitting?"

There was no answer from Freddy Farmer for a couple of seconds. Dave watched the two Wacos come rushing down in almost a vertical dive. Instinctively he slid his hand up the control stick and took off the safety catch of the firing button.

"Eh, what?" came Freddy Farmer's sudden reply. "Pull off and leave the blighters? Leave them perhaps to get somebody else like poor Tracey? Not a bit of it, Dave. Let's give it to the beggars, and give it to them good!"

"Words right out of my mouth!" Dave cried gayly. "And to make sure it's no mistake, we'll let them smack out the first burst. I still wonder where Colonel Welsh's agent is. Too bad he's going to miss this!"

"His hard luck," Freddy grunted. "But he isn't here, so he isn't here, and that's that. He—
On guard, Dave!"

The last wasn't necessary. Dawson hadn't taken his eyes off the diving Wacos for so much as a split second. Even as Freddy yelled, he saw twin jetting streams of orange red flame come spurting out the nose of the leading plane. And in that same split second he slammed his weight on the Vultee's controls and sent the Air Corps ship cartwheeling off to the left and up as though it had been slapped by a bolt of lightning.

So unexpected and so swift had been his maneuver that when he yanked the Vultee out of it a good thousand feet higher in the air, the two Wacos were still diving earthward and still spitting out bullets from all their guns. A harsh laugh rattled off Dave's lips as he kicked rudder and dropped the nose a hair.

"Go back to flight training school, chumps!" he shouted. "Who do you think we are—a couple of two hour solo cadets? Here! Here are a few kisses from Uncle Sam!"

As Dave spoke the last he sticked the nearest of the two Wacos into his sights and jabbed the electric trigger button. His two forward fixed guns yammered out flame and sound, and the Waco suddenly acted as though its pilot had flown it straight into a meat grinder. The left wings came off clean as a whistle. The fuselage buckled in the middle, and smoke and flame belched out from under the engine cowling, and went whirling backward to envelop the plane completely. Dave watched it closely, but when no figure tumbled down out of that smoke to become a man dangling at the ends of parachute shroud lines, he shuddered slightly and licked his suddenly dry lips.

"Tough!" he muttered, "even if he is an Axis rat. But he asked for it. And he had the chance to get in the first licks, too!"

Hardly had the last left Dave's lips before Freddy Farmer's rear guns spoke their piece. The second Waco had come out of its wild dive, and its pilot—perhaps a little jarred by the sudden death of his flying mate—had tried the absolutely crazy maneuver of cutting around and getting in under the Vultee's tail. With a sharpshooter like Freddy Farmer, that maneuver was just about as sane an effort as stepping out a ten story window and trying to walk across the air to a building on the other side of the street.

The English youth's rear guns slapped out no more than a two second burst each. But that was more than enough. It was as though a giant's steel fist crashed down, and one ripped up, and the Waco were caught between the two. The biplane simply came apart at the seams and the pieces were showered all over the place. Unlike the other Waco pilot, however, the second Waco pilot managed to get away with his life. Both Dave and Freddy saw him arc out from the shower of wreckage as though shot from the mouth of a cannon. A moment later, though, as he went slowly spinning head over heels downward, a puff of white shot up past his head. And in another moment he was swinging like a clock's pendulum at the ends of taut shroud lines. Dave glanced back at Freddy and nodded.

"Nice shooting, Freddy!" he cried. "Help yourself to a cigar, my little man!"

"You didn't miss, yourself!" the English youth shouted back. Then, casting his eye down at the dangling parachutist, he muttered, "At times like this I almost wish I were a Nazi. Then I could do plain murder, and it wouldn't come back to me in my dreams. That lucky blighter will probably be up to more dirty Axis business tomorrow."

"No, not tomorrow!" Dave echoed as he stared downward. "He's got one awful long walk out of those mountains. And if you must know how I feel about it, I kind of hope that he doesn't make it, if you get what I mean."

"I do," Freddy said grimly. "And the feeling is mutual. I see that our light plane friend isn't around. As soon as his work was completed he got away in a hurry. How about tooting around a bit to see if we can pick up the beggar? I'd at least like to give him the scare of his rotten life."

"I'd like to give him just a little more than that!" Dave echoed as he cast his narrow eyed gaze about the surrounding air. "But I guess we'll have to pass up that little pleasure. I don't see hide nor hair of him, and we've got places to go, anyway. Well, Freddy how's for handing me that fur-lined propeller I won?"

"Fur what?" Farmer gasped. "What are you raving about?"

"Colonel Welsh's tapped phone lines!" Dave said, and grinned at him. "Kind of close to being right, wasn't I?"

"You modest blighter!" Freddy snapped.

"When will you learn your manners, and wait for praise to come, instead of asking for it?"

"Who, me?" Dawson chuckled. "Wait for praise from a jealous guy like you? And get it maybe when my beard is way down to here, and I'm in a wheel chair? Not a chance! But thanks for them kind words, pal! After all, it was just a hunch. I could have been wrong."

"Not a bit of it!" Freddy cried, and then grinned. "I knew definitely that you were right, because, you see, I suspected those phone lines being tapped long before you even thought of it. I knew how pleased you'd be to bring it up, so I simply remained silent. That's how it really was, old thing."

"Okay, okay!" Dave groaned, and gave a sad shake of his head. "We're both a couple of very wonderful guys. Let's leave it like that, huh?"

"Oh, quite!" Freddy said, and then, giving his right hand a snap wave, he added, "And now, my good man, stop wasting Government high octane. Take me to my destination, and be quick about it, will you? I've much more important things to do than sit here chitchatting with the likes of you— Hey, there!"

When Freddy shouted out the last he was upside down and hanging on his safety harness, and clutching at the sides of the cockpit for support. Grinning back at him like an ape, Dave whipped the Vultee back onto even keel and banked southeast again.

"Quite, quite, my lord!" he chirped. "Lovely weather for flying, isn't it? The air as smooth as a mill pond. Oh, yes, yes, and pip-pip, old tin of fruit!"

Freddy Farmer was unable to make any reply. He was still struggling to get back his breath, and swallow his heart into place.

CHAPTER NINE

Whispering Bullets

THE SUN WAS a glittering bronz disc in the heavens when Dave eased back the throttle and sent the Vultee coasting down toward the surface of the Albuquerque Air Corps Base. The rest of the trip had been completely uneventful. It had been nothing but a scenic joyride that both boys had enjoyed to the limit. But now that Albuquerque was down there their minds put aside the beauty of the trip and came back to more serious things. One attempt on their lives had been made. Would there be another at Albuquerque? Also, would Colonel Welsh's agents at Albuquerque have anything new to report? The Chief of U. S. Intelligence had not described his two agents at Albuquerque, but both Dave and Freddy would know them instantly—that is, when the identifying sentence was spoken to them.

As he guided the ship down Dave impulsively slipped a hand into his pocket and pulled out the slightly gashed copper coin he had taken from the dead Tracey. Colonel Welsh had given

it to him just before they went out to the Frisco
Air Base. He had also given one to Freddy Farmer. It was, Colonel Welsh had explained, a
special SOS signal for U. S. Intelligence agents
located in and around the Canal Zone. It identified its holder as a member of the Service, and
all agents seeing it were to drop whatever they
were doing and lend instant assistance, regardless. When found on the body of a wounded
man, the copper disc was a silent order for the
wounded man to receive medical assistance at
once—as he might possess valuable military information that approaching death was striving
to cheat him out of delivering.

Dave fingered the silver-filled copper disc,
and stared down at it thoughtfully.

"I hope I never have to flash you," he
grunted. "You're certainly no lucky charm. Not
to poor Tracey, you weren't. Yet—you did tell
Colonel Welsh who Tracey was, didn't you?
Well, here's hoping you don't have to tell him
the same thing—about me. And how!"

"I say!" Freddy Farmer suddenly screamed
in his ear. "Land on the field, not *under* it, will
you?"

Dave snapped his gaze front, gulped, and
eased up the nose of the Vultee. He was uncon-

sciously coming in very "hot," and the surface of the field was much closer than he'd realized, so absorbed had he been with his thoughts about the copper disc.

"Just giving you an extra thrill, free of charge, pal!" he shouted back to Freddy. "Always aim to please the customer, you know. Okay! Mother Earth coming up. End of the line. There! Was that to your liking, sir?"

Dave settled the Vultee in a beautiful three-point, and gently braked it to a full stop. He sat there for a moment with his eyes on the Operations Tower. He got the flash to taxi in and sent the Vultee trundling along and down the cross runway toward the seemingly mile-long tarmac lined in back by an equally long row of massive hangars.

He finally slipped the Vultee in between a couple of bombers and killed the engine.

"I mean it, this time," he said, turning around to Freddy. "End of the line, and all out. But sit here, if you like. Me, I'm going to report to the check-in officer, and then get me a bottle of pop, or something."

Freddy Farmer brightened and scrambled down from his cockpit.

"I say, do you suppose I could get a spot of

'tea?" he asked.

Dave frowned and looked at him. In fact, he cocked his head first on one side, and then on the other.

"What size skirt do you take, and blouse?" he murmured, straight-faced. "As a girl you'd get it easy. These guys are very polite. But to ask for tea in that uniform, with pilot's wings and all—"

Dave paused and sighed heavily. Freddy glared and took a quick step forward.

"That, my good fellow, is the last straw!" he cried. "Now your countrymen here will see what happens to a bloke who insults the honored and traditional drink of the English. I shall—"

Freddy stopped as a couple of mechanics came running over to the plane. They came to a halt and saluted.

"The check-in booth is over there, sir," one of them said to Dave. "If you hurry, you'll make it by two ofter one. We'll take charge of your ship, sir. Nice trip?"

Two after one! Those three words were like three bombshells going off in Dave's brain. They were the code words that would identify Colonel Welsh's two agents who would meet them in Albuquerque. But only one, the taller, had spoken them. Dave looked at the shorter one and smiled apologetically, and touched a finger to his ear.

"Engine deafened me a little," he said. "What was that?"

"The check-in booth, sir," the shorter of the two mechanics said. "It's close to two after one. You'd better step on it."

Dave grinned and winked.

"Right," he said. Then, arching one brow, "And after we've checked in?"

"You can remember something you left in the ship," the tall mechanic said. "We'll both be here wiping her off. Was it a quiet trip?"

"Not for two Waco pilots, it wasn't," Dave said grimly, and beckoned a finger at Freddy Farmer. "See you soon."

"That's the pair, right enough!" Freddy breathed softly as he and Dave headed over to the check-in booth. "And did you see how your news startled them?"

"As I remember, it startled us, too!" Dave said with a chuckle. "Come on, step on it! I want to get back and find out if those two have learned anything new."

Freddy quickened his step to keep pace with Dave, and together they hurried over to the check-in hut and through the door. A young Air Corps lieutenant looked up from a desk and greeted them with a smile.

"Sign here, Captains," he said, and pushed a loose-leaf book across the desk. "Passing through, or are you reporting for duty?"

"Passing through," Dave said as he signed his name, and gave the pen to Freddy. "Have any orders come through while we've been in the air?"

The young Air Corps lieutenant swung the book around, looked at the two names, and shook his head.

"No sir," he said. "Nothing for either of you. We received word you'd taken off from Frisco Base. You landed on the way down?"

"No, why?" Dave asked.

The young lieutenant grinned and nodded his head at the clock.

"A Vultee is a pretty fast ship, Captain," he said.

Dave frowned, and then suddenly the light dawned.

"Oh, sure, I get it," he said. "We went sightseeing. This is my Chinese friend's first visit to this country. I took a little time out to give him a good look."

The young Air Corps lieutenant was staring puzzle-eyed at Freddy Farmer as the two aces walked out of the office. Outside, Dave took a quick step away from Freddy, and waited for his pal to go into action. But Freddy just kept on walking.

"Be calm, old thing," Freddy said quietly. "That was a compliment you paid me. The Chinese are a wonderful people. They've been proving it to the world for the last five years. So, trot along with me, my funny boy. I won't hurt you."

"Smack-o!" Dave grunted as he flushed a little. "I guess that one sort of upped and backfired in my face. Darn right the Chinese are okay. Let's forget the whole thing, huh?"

"Done with, already," Freddy grinned. "And how about *you* stepping on it this time? I'm anxious to hear what those two agents of Colonel Welsh's have to say. But I can't say they look much like agents."

"And just what does an agent look like?" Dave chuckled.

"Oh, rather homely looking," Freddy said. "Flat-headed, flat feet, and bow legs. Just an ordinary horrible looking chap. You're an agent, aren't you—of a sort?"

"Why, oh why do I keep opening my big mouth?" Dave wailed. "That's twice in as many minutes. You're catching on too fast, my little man."

"Could be I was really ahead at the start, you know?" the English youth shot back at him.

Dave made noises in his throat and clamped his lips shut tight. In silence the pair walked the rest of the way to where the two Intelligence agents in mechanics' garb were wiping off the wings of the Vultee. When Dave and Freddy came up they continued wiping the wings, but both edged over so that they could talk in low tones without appearing to be talking at all from more than fifty feet away.

"What's that about the two Wacos?" the tall one asked. "What happened?"

Dave bent over to inspect a section of the wing and in rapid sentences told of the little adventure on the way down. The two mechanics whistled softly and shot both Dave and Freddy looks of frank admiration.

"I say, anything new at this end?" Freddy murmured.

"Nothing yet," replied the shorter of the other two. "We've checked and rechecked, but as yet we haven't got a nibble."

"Nibble?" Freddy echoed, and frowned in perplexity.

"An idea of who, and how, about Tracey," the mechanic explained. "And—well, the two of us feel like going out and cutting our throats."

"And *how,* we do!" grated the taller mechanic. "Of course we didn't know who he was. It's part of our job to meet all foreign ships landing here. I mean, planes that don't belong to this field. We met Tracey's ship, and we serviced it for him. If I had only known, I'd have watched it like a hawk until he'd taken off again. But we didn't know a thing about him until a couple of hours ago when Colonel Welsh got us on the wire to explain about you two coming down. He didn't tell us where you were headed, just that you were two after one, and that those were to be the identification words."

The man looked questioningly at Dave, but the Yank ace just grinned, and shrugged.

"Oh, we're just out for a bit of fishing, you know," Freddy Farmer offered the information presently. "We're hoping we have all kinds of luck."

"I'm hoping for you," the tall agent mechanic said. "We both are. That means you're just passing through, huh? When do you want your ship ready? And I guess we might as well patch up those two bullet holes."

The last caused Dave almost to jump out of his shoes.

"Huh?" he gulped, bug-eyed. "Bullet holes? Where?"

The tall mechanic pointed to the left side of the fuselage at a point exactly between the forward and rear pits. There were two neat bullet holes in the dural covering, not over an inch apart. Dave stared at them and felt beads of sweat break out on his forehead. A foot farther front and they would have been in his spine. A foot farther to the rear and they would have been in Freddy's legs.

"Holy smoke!" he breathed. "Sweet tripe! I had no idea!"

"Take a good look, and remember it, old thing!" Freddy Farmer said dryly. "Next time don't be so blasted heroic, and give the other bloke first cracks. Don't give him first cracks at all."

"Don't rub it in!" Dave growled. "Besides, I couldn't open fire on them first. We weren't sure about them until they started shooting."

"Yes, that's true," Freddy said as a sort of

apology. "But just the same, don't give the next bloke the same kind of opportunity."

Dave shrugged and turned to the taller of the two mechanics.

"We're heading south," he said. "Just where, you can guess. When we leave depends on the Commandant here at Albuquerque. We won't be taking this Vultee. But getting back to poor Tracey, did you happen to see anybody hanging around near his ship? Did you see much of him? I mean, we got the idea that he discovered somebody was on his tail, and sort of kept out of sight while he was here. Do you know if that's right?"

The two agents, serving at Albuquerque as mechanics, frowned in deep thought, and then exchanged glances at each other.

"If we'd only known who Tracey was, we'd have kept our eyes open," the tall mechanic said, and gave a little shake of his head. "It so happened, though, we did see him around and about a couple of times. He was with the field Commandant, Major Larkin, for a while. And we saw him with a couple of the pilots, whom he seemed to know. He told us that he was pulling out of here first thing in the morning. But it wasn't until close to noon when he appeared on the field. Naturally, we didn't ask any questions. As I've said, we didn't know a thing—then."

"I wish we had!" the shorter of the two mechanics muttered. "He didn't look so hot to me. I mean, I thought he'd had a big night with the boys, and had cracked his head on something. He had a fair sized piece of plaster on his forehead over his left eye. He certainly didn't look so good. But of course we didn't say a thing."

Dave Dawson was silent for a moment. His brain was turning back in memory to those moments he had spent with the dying Tracey in that desolate mountain valley. He remembered the gash on the man's forehead. The surgeon's plaster had probably been torn off in the crash. At the time, though, Dave had believed the head injury to have been caused by the crash.

"So an attack was made on him here?" he murmured more to himself than the others. "That's pretty positive. But he survived it, so somebody—probably the same rat—doctored his oxygen tank, knowing that he'd go for altitude to get over the mountains. Maybe this is a dumb question, but who here would know he was headed for Frisco Air Base?"

"Any number of people, I'm afraid," the tall mechanic replied with a shrug. "The check-in officer, the Commandant, the operations officer, and—well, any of the pilots he happened to mention it to. Why? Anything special behind that question?"

"Just grabbing at straws," Dave said with a sigh. "It's pretty certain that somebody here, who knew his take-off time, sent word to Frisco, so that the rat, or rats, at the Frisco end could check and make sure."

"What's that, Dave?" Freddy Farmer spoke up with a frown. "Why did anybody in Frisco have to know, if the poor chap's oxygen tank was fixed up?"

"To make sure the tank *did* knock him out and make him crash, and die," Dawson replied grimly. "It wouldn't gain them much to make that sneak attack on Rigby's office if Tracey were going to make contact with Colonel Welsh, anyway."

"Yes, that's true," Freddy nodded. "So some blighter here who knew his take-off time is our man, or at least one of them."

"Sure," Dave grunted, and made a sweep of his hand that took in the entire Base. "So take your pick. The old needle in a hay stack, Freddy. A dead end street, I'd say. Well, I guess we'd better report to Major Larkin, and find out how soon we're leaving."

"Yes, that would be a good idea," the taller of the two agents replied. "But here's a tip. If you're staying here for the night, don't go for any walks in the dark. I think it would be wise to stick in the officers' mess, and relax, if you get what I mean."

"I guess I do," Dave grunted, and gave the tall one a searching look. "Somebody *we* don't know *knows* that we have arrived, eh?"

"Yes, that's the idea," the tall mechanic said with a faint grin. "We realize now that Tracey didn't bump his head into any door while he was having a good time with some of his pilot friends."

"Not a chance!" the shorter mechanic said grimly. "My guess is that he got popped at. Whispering bullets in the dark. And it wouldn't be the first time, either. The rats we're up against always deal from the bottom of the deck. So watch your step. And of course, we'll be watching you."

"That's a deal," Dave said, and gave them a friendly grin. "If we stay the night we won't do any sight-seeing after dark. Well, we'll be seeing you again. So long, for now."

CHAPTER TEN

Freddy Stubs His Toe

MAJOR LARKIN, Commandant of the Albuquerque Air Base, was the kind of a man who looked as if he had been cut out of solid granite, and fitted up with coiled steel springs. And under the silver wings on his tunic was a row of decoration ribbons that proved he was also the kind of a man who lived up to his looks. But the smile of greeting he gave to Dave and Freddy was genuine enough, and his hand shake was warm and friendly.

"Assigned for duty with the Ninety-Sixth in the Canal Zone, eh?" he said, and tapped the official orders on his desk. "Well, that's a great spot for flying. A fine bunch of boys down there, too. Wish I were going along with you. Well, get an extra U-boat for me, will you?"

"We'll do our best, sir," Dave said with a grin. "And—well, when do we leave, sir?"

"Anxious to get going, eh?" the Base Commandant echoed with a chuckle. "Well, tomorrow morning. A half dozen ferry bombers are sitting down here for refueling tomorrow. Then from here to Brownsville, Texas. And then the water jump to the Canal Zone. Will that be okey with you two? That's the fastest service I can give you, to the Canal Zone by ferry bomber."

Dave and Freddy exchanged startled glances. It wasn't usual for high ranking officers to ask if such and such a thing were okay. Major Larkin saw the exchange of looks and chuckled softly.

"I read all the papers, and of course the communiques," he said with a twinkle in his eyes. "Seems to me I recall something about two lads named Dawson and Farmer doing a pretty good job against the Japs trying to break up that Marshall Islands show we had a while back. And I think I remember, too, that long before that those same two did all right on a couple of R.A.F. Intelligence jobs. But of course, it could have been two other fellows."

Dave and Freddy grinned, and then Dave nodded.

"That's right, sir," he said. "It was two other fellows. We're joining Ninety-Six to take a couple cracks at U-boats in the Caribbean."

"Don't worry, your secret is safe, whatever it is," Major Larkin laughed. Then, as his face became just a little grave, he said, "But I wish you all the luck in the world with those—U-boats. I'm not connected with Intelligence, but rumors get around, you know. It's an odds-on bet that something is going to pop down there. I only hope and pray that you and the others will be able to slap the cover on pronto."

"We'll do our best, sir," Dave repeated mechanically. "But as you never can tell what will be a help, I'd like to ask, what about the rumors you've heard, sir? Anything special about any of them?"

The Albuquerque Base Commandant scowled out the window of his office, and absently cracked the knuckles of his left hand with his right.

"Nothing that isn't public property," he said. "Just the usual rumors about an impending attack on the Canal."

"Why, sir?" Freddy asked. "Why an *impending* attack on the Canal?"

"An obvious military operation," the Major replied with a gesture. "And impending because it hasn't been made long before this. That Canal isn't closed up for the duration, you know. We're making twenty-four hour a day use of it. And it isn't a bunch of canoes that are going through it on their way to Australia, and India, and the

Middle East."

"Then you think the Japs are planning an-other Pearl Harbor in the Canal Zone, sir?" Freddy pressed.

The Major looked at him and grinned.

"What do you think?" he countered. "They'd certainly love to cut that section of the supply line, wouldn't they?"

"Oh, quite, sir," Freddy said with a nod. Then, after a moment's hesitation, he added, "But I'm afraid, sir, that I don't agree with you."

"He's like that, sir," Dave said with a chuckle. "An awful stubborn guy with his ideas. And you'd be surprised how often he hits the nail on the head. Yes, sir! Freddy's a whole lot more than just a pukka fighting pilot."

"Oh, I say, drop it, will you!" Freddy growled as a flush flooded his cheeks. "Every-body has ideas and opinions of his own, you know. What Dawson really means, sir, is that I haven't sense enough to keep mine to myself. But we must be taking up your valuable time, sir."

"Not a bit of it!" Major Larkin said, giving Freddy a searching look. "You don't agree with me, so that makes me curious. I'd like to know your opinion, really. Why don't you think the Japs would like to close the Canal?"

"I didn't say that, sir," the English born ace replied quickly. "They'd love to, no end. I simply mean that they wouldn't attempt it. Too far to come, too great a cost for the small amount of damage they'd do. It stands to reason that you Americans aren't ever going to let another Pearl Harbor happen any place. Oh, the Japs would love to do it, but they can't. And I fancy they know that better than we do."

"Then, personally, you don't expect any attack on the Canal?" Major Larkin murmured with a smile. "The rumors are just hot air?"

"On the contrary, I do expect an attack, sir," Freddy Farmer said soberly. "But not by the Japs. By the Nazis. In a way they have far more to gain by such an attack than the Japs."

"How's that?" Dave broke in. "Make that a little clearer, will you, Freddy?"

"Oh, never mind," the English youth said, and shrugged. "It's just a lot of words, and probably not very interesting, or enlightening. Let's get going, shall we, Dave?"

"Not yet," Major Larkin said with a grin. "I'm giving you an order, Captain Farmer. Answer Dawson's question. I want to hear it."

"Well, sir," Freddy began, after fixing his eyes on a point on the desk, and holding them there, "the answer is Russia, in my humble opinion. Hitler wants Japan to attack Russia from the east. Such an attack would simplify his problem enormously. But before Japan will tackle that kind of a job, Hitler has got to show that he in turn will help Japan. He's been doing it a little with his intensified U-boat campaign along the Atlantic seaboard, and in the Carribbean. But that is not enough, and—well, perhaps Japan has told him so. It is Japan who is holding large British forces in India, forces that could be well used in Egypt. Before Japan does anything more to help Hitler, the Nips want something in return from him. So—the Panama Canal. If Hitler can plug that up he will have done Japan a tremendously important favor. That's the way I look at it. . . . But I say! Let's drop this, shall we? I'm probably just talking silly rot."

"You aren't, Farmer," Major Larkin said, and gave him a look of frank admiration. "And you are most certainly one of the reasons!"

Freddy looked puzzled, and blinked.

"Reasons, sir?" he echoed.

Major Larkin smiled and nodded.

"Exactly," he said. "One of the reasons why there'll always be an England! Well, I'll be seeing you two later at mess."

The two youths saluted and went outside into the sunshine. Freddy's face was on fire with a blush, but there was an intensely pleased look in his eyes. Dave glanced sidewise at him and chuckled softly.

"So you won't talk, huh?" he grunted. "Boy! Did you lay the words right down the groove! Pal, I'm right proud of you, I am!"

"Oh, come off it!" Freddy growled, but the pleased smile was still on his lips. "Major Larkin's probably laughing his head off, right now."

"No he isn't," Dave said solemnly. "And neither am I. As I remarked in there, you usually smack the nail right on the head. And I think you got dead center again this time. It was okay, Freddy. There's just one question you didn't answer. And I sure wish you would. It would help you and me a lot to know the answer."

"And the question?" Freddy demanded, and shot him a suspicious look. "An impossible one to answer, no doubt?"

"How—" Dave said, and there was no kidding in his face—"how do they figure to plug up the Canal?"

"An impossible question, as I suspected," Freddy said, but there was no scorn in his voice. "Yes, how? And will we find out?"

Dave's lips came together to form a thin grim line. He unconsciously clenched his two fists and squinted narrow-eyed ahead.

"We'll find out!" he grated softly. "We've got to! But—but will we find out *in time!* Seven-Eleven. You know, Freddy, I don't think I've ever wanted to meet anybody as much as I want to meet this mysterious bird they call Seven-Eleven!"

"Quite, me too!" the English youth answered. "But speaking of meeting people, right now I'd much rather meet the mess cook here. Feel like I haven't eaten for hours. What say we try to get a bite or two of lunch, eh?"

"Freddy Farmer of the mile wide, and deep, stomach!" Dave sighed. "Okay, or you'll be weeping on my shoulder from here on in. That's the Officer's Mess over there. Chase along. I'll be with you in a couple of minutes. It just occurred to me that we'd better let Colonel Welsh know that we've arrived. Probably those two agents of his will tell him. But I'll trot over and tell them to be sure to do that little thing."

"Right-o," Freddy said. "And I say, take a final look in both cockpits, just to see if we left anything behind, will you?"

"That, too," Dave said with a nod, and swerved over toward the hangar line.

When he reached the Vultee the two agent-mechanics were nowhere to be seen. He climbed up and had a good look into both cockpits, but he failed to find anything that belonged to either Freddy or himself. Then, on second thought, he began giving the entire plane and engine a thorough look-see inspection to see if other lucky bullets had done it any damage. He felt very guilty about the two bullet holes in the fuselage, and he wanted to make sure that the plane wouldn't be returned to its owner with any other damage that had been overlooked.

A fifteen minute inspection, however, brought to light no further evidence of the air battle, so he turned away and headed over to the check-in office. The young Air Corps lieutenant wasn't there. A sergeant was in charge, and he gave Dave a respectful nod as the pilot entered.

"Yes, Captain?" he inquired politely.

"Captain Farmer and I just pulled in from Frisco Base," Dave said. "I'd like word sent back that we arrived. Do you send that sort of thing out, or do I go to the operations officer?"

"We send it out from here, sir," the sergeant said. Then, after thumbing through his book of records, he added, "Frisco has been notified, Captain. Half an hour ago, by Second Lieutenant Miller, who was on duty."

"Okay, thanks," Dave said with a grin, and turned away. "I just wanted to be sure that—"

He cut the rest off short as he heard the clanging of the field ambulance bell. He turned all the way around and snapped a look out onto the field. There wasn't any crash out there, nor was there any plane coming in that looked as if it were in trouble. He shrugged, made a face at his own nervousness and started down the hangar line toward the Officers' Mess. It wasn't until he had passed a line of bombers that he was able to see the ambulance. It had come to a stop in front of the Officers' Mess. There was a small group of uniformed men gathered about.

An eerie feeling of terror suddenly struck Dave, and he broke into a run. He pounded over the one hundred and fifty yards of flying field ground in less time than it takes to tell about it. When he reached the fringe of the group and peered past them and down at the huddled figure on the ground, his heart shot up into his mouth and choked off the cry that tried to get by. It was Freddy Farmer on the ground. His eyes were closed, his face was white, and there was blood on the left side of his head just above the ear. One look, and then Dave was through the group and on his knees beside Freddy.

"What happened?" he demanded of anybody who might have the answer.

"I'm not sure," spoke up a pilot captain who had just a touch of grey in his otherwise jet black hair. "I was just coming out of the Mess, and saw him headed over this way at a pretty fast clip. He tripped on a stone, started to save himself, and then spun around and went flat as something smacked him. Looks like a bullet crease to me."

"And not bad," said a field medico in white. "Just nicked him, fortunately. Look, he's coming around now. Hold still, son. Just relax while I swab this a bit and stick something on it."

Freddy had opened his eyes, and was trying to struggle up, but the field medico gently forced him back on the ground, and went to work on the bullet crease. Freddy's eyes met Dave's, but he didn't seem to recognize his pal for a second or two. Then recognition came in a flash, and he grinned.

"Hello, Dave," he said. "What happened? What am I doing here?"

"By rights you should be praying your thankfulness," Dave told him with a grin. "It seems you got clipped by a bullet. But you had stubbed your toe first. That saved you. How do you feel"

"Why, right as rain!" Freddy replied, and gave the medico an annoyed look. "A bit of an ache, but that's all. A bullet, you say? What bullet, and who shot at me?"

"Nobody shot at you, I don't guess," the jet black-haired pilot captain said with a smile. "We've got a rifle and pistol target range over there. I guess it was a ricochet bullet that nicked you. But that still makes you one lucky lad. And I'm not kidding!"

"A ricochet" Dave echoed sharply, and stared at the pilot hard. "You mean this sort of thing happens often?"

"No, I don't mean it happens often!" the other replied, and returned his steady stare. "It hasn't happened once in the year I've been here. What are you driving at? You think somebody took a deliberate shot at your buddy?"

Dave popped open his mouth, but checked

what he wanted to say in time. Instead, he grinned and shook his head.

"No, of course not," he said. "We only just arrived. Don't know anybody here. Why should anybody?"

"That's what I mean," the other pilot captain grinned, and gestured with his hands.

By then the medico had finished with Freddy, and helped him up on his feet. As soon as he was upright the color came back into Freddy's face, and he seemed none the worse for his little adventure—that is, save for the patch on the side of his head over his left ear.

"Just take it easy for a little while, Captain, and you'll be as good as new," the medico advised. Then with a grin as he dumped his stuff into his bag and snapped it shut, "Sorry I couldn't give you a ride. Maybe next time, though."

"Thank you, no!" Freddy grinned back at him. "I detest ambulances. Something too definite about them, you know."

"And how I know!" the medico grunted, and climbed into the ambulance. "Well, it broke the routine, anyway."

The ambulance drove away, and the group slowly broke up, leaving Dave and Freddy alone.

"Well, shall we eat, eh?" Freddy said.

"You're okay, that's a cinch," Dave growled, but softened it with a grin. "But, boy! My heart's just going back into place. Let's get out of the open spaces. A ricochet? Nuts! Somebody on that target range got off the target quite a bit, and took a bead on you, Freddy."

"I think so, too!" the English youth replied as his eyes flashed fire. "Never mind lunch. Let's go hunt out the blighter. I've got a bit I could say to him—and do, too!"

"No, we eat," Dave said firmly, and took hold of Freddy's arm. "It stands to reason he's not there waiting for us. And the sooner we get under cover, the better. No sense inviting pot shots. But I'm sure thankful you have big feet!"

"I'll remember that when I get my strength back!" Freddy Farmer snapped, and allowed Dave to lead him into the Officers' Mess.

CHAPTER ELEVEN

Flames Of Doom

WITH HER FOUR Wright "Cyclone" engines thundering out their synchronized song of power, the giant Boeing B-17 Flying Fortress lifted clear of the Albuquerque Air Base runway and nosed up for altitude and the start of the nine hundred odd mile flight to Brownsville, Texas. Back aft by the middle bomb bay, Dave Dawson and Freddy Farmer relaxed comfortably and watched the falling ground through one of the side ports.

"Nice!" Dave grunted. "This is the life, at times. Let somebody else do the flying for a change, hey, Freddy?"

"A fine thing to ask me!" Freddy snorted. "I'm usually a passenger anyway. But it does make a chap feel good not to have any flight responsibility for a change. These are certainly wonderful airplanes."

"Plenty good, plenty good," Dave agreed. "I bet before long that Hitler will shoot anybody who mentions 'Flying Fortress' in his presence. And the day will come, too, and soon, when these babies will be regarded as the smaller type of bomber. We'll have six and eight engine jobs dumping them off on Adolf's head. But, by the way, during all the rush this morning I forgot to ask you how the old head was. You look okay from here."

"I'm fine," the English youth replied with a smile. "Had a restless night, though. No pain. Just dreams, crazy ones. I dreamed that little cross-eyed men were shooting at me from all directions, and not missing by much."

"But they missed, like that rat yesterday," Dave murmured, and squinted down back at the Albuquerque Base that was fast losing itself in the general landscape. "In a way I'm sorry to leave Albuquerque. I mean, it's sort of like unfinished business. There's a dirty rat down there, and we didn't even get close to him. He knows we were there, and he knows we've taken off for Brownsville. But there's one thing in our favor—if you could call it that."

"And you mean?" Freddy Farmer prompted when the Yank air ace lapsed into silence and didn't continue. "Go on, finish it."

"We've at least got them worried," Dave finally said, and nodded for grim emphasis. "Colonel Welsh's faked message to Washington

H.Q. has got them standing on their ears. They think we know something mighty important, when in truth we don't know a darn thing. And that little fact has me standing on my ear, if you must know."

"I'm with you there," Freddy sighed, and gave a little shake of his head. "And if you must know, I'm more than a little worried. I mean, things have happened, but—well, not a thing to our advantage."

"We're still alive and kicking," Dave reminded him. "You could class that as an advantage."

"Oh, I do!" Freddy said instantly. "Quite! But apart from still being alive, what have we gained? Nothing. Absolutely nothing. And to get down to brass tacks, as you Yanks say, what have we ahead?"

"Who knows?" Dave grunted, and shrugged. "We'll just have to stay in and pitch, and hope for a break. But there is Second Lieutenant Marble with the Ninety-Sixth Attack Squadron. He's our ace card, you know. All this business just leads up to him. You might say that now we're just running the gantlet of enemy agents, who are trying to cut us down. But Marble is at the end, and when we get to him—"

Dave finished the rest by winking and snapping his fingers. Freddy Farmer nodded, but the expression on his face indicated that he was not very much impressed.

"Yes, quite so," he murmured. "But, supposing Marble can't help us any? Supposing he doesn't know a thing about what poor Tracey was working on? What then?"

"Then we know for sure we've got to start from scratch," Dave said quietly. "And, Freddy, I've been thinking."

"Good lad," the English youth said with a smile. "Splendid! You'll be surprised in how many ways it will improve you!"

"Nuts, I'm serious!" Dave snapped. "I've been doing an awful lot of thinking about poor Tracey. There is the key, Freddy. Poor Tracey. No matter how much I try to get away from it, I keep coming back to the firm belief that he gave us the key to the whole business, in those four words that we think added up to Albuquerque."

"You don't think so, now?" Freddy asked.

"I don't know what to think!" Dawson muttered savagely. "He probably was just pronouncing Albuquerque slowly so's we'd be sure to get it. But why? Tell me why."

"I haven't the faintest idea," Freddy replied with an unhappy shake of his head.

"So that's what gets me," Dave said. "Why use his last bit of strength to tell us to tell Colonel Welsh that he came from Albuquerque, when Colonel Welsh already knew that? And that word, southern? Why southern Albuquerque? It doesn't make sense, Freddy. I'm darned afraid that we didn't get it right, that we muffed what was really the key to this whole mystery."

"Well, now that you bring it up," Freddy Farmer said slowly, "I must confess that I haven't been at all satisfied with our deductions on what he said. But he repeated it several times, and it sounded the same each time."

"I know," Dave said heavily. "But let's both keep it in our minds. I have a hunch that we were all wet on that. I think that something will come to us out of the blue, and then poor Tracey's dying words will make sense."

"Well, there's still Second Lieutenant Marble," Freddy Farmer grunted. "I refuse, though, to let my hopes get too high about him. But of course there is a chance that he can explain a lot of things, or at least enough for us to get working on."

The two youths lapsed into mutual silence

and were content with their own thoughts as the big Flying Fortress drilled its way through the air toward Brownsville. As a matter of fact, neither of them spoke for some fifteen minutes or so, and then only when the big bomber's Flight Engineer came past them on his way aft.

"Anything we can do to help, Lieutenant Kelley?" Dave asked with a smile. "We sort of feel as if we were cheating on the job, just sitting back here and taking it easy."

The Flight Engineer paused for a moment and grinned down at him.

"No, there isn't a thing, thanks," he said. "Glad to have you two aboard for company. These ferrying jobs are pretty dry. I'm just about to rustle up some coffee, and a sandwich or two. Can I interest you?"

"Oh, quite!" Freddy Farmer said, and beamed. "I say, that would be splendid. This American air, you know, makes me frightfully hungry quite often."

"Quite often, he says!" Dave groaned. "He really means no more than twenty-four hours a day. You don't happen to have a whole cow aboard for him to nibble on, do you, just as a little snack in between his regular meals? But I could go for a cup of java. Here, let me give you a hand with the business."

Dave scrambled up on his feet and followed the Flight Engineer past the flare chute compartment and further aft to the bomber's galley. They had the little electric stove going in nothing flat, and it was not long after that before the pleasing aroma of coffee was mingling with the one hundred and one equally pleasant (to pilots) smells inside the bomber. Freddy sliced bread and Dave buttered it, and the Flight Engineer got out the various things to put in between the buttered slices. It was when he was cutting the first sandwich cornerwise that he suddenly straightened up and sniffed.

"What's that smell, or is it my imagination?" he asked.

"I smell nothing but nice things to eat," was Freddy Farmer's reply to the question.

Dave didn't make any reply for a moment. He sniffed hard and was suddenly conscious of a very strange smell in his nose. And it didn't come from the cook stove, either. He tried to identify the smell, but the best he could do was to guess it was burning rubber, or the smell of scorched paint.

"I get something," he grunted, and turned to look forward. "It smells something like—"

The last froze on Dave's lips, and for a second or two he couldn't move, let alone speak. Just forward at the front end of the flare compartment a tiny thread of yellowish smoke was seeping out under a locker door. Even as he stared a tongue of blue white flame licked out. And there was instantly a hissing sound in the inside of the bomber.

"Fire!" Dave yelped, and snapped out of his trance. "Something's going up close to the flare compartment!"

Even as Dave spoke the words he was in full action. With a single sweep of his hand he grabbed one of the many placed special fire extinguishers down off the galley wall, and bounded forward. He was but a few steps from the yellow smoke curling up from under the locker door when suddenly a sharp explosion blew the door off its metal hinges. Instantly the whole interior of that part of the bomber was filled with flashing light and acrid yellow smoke that choked and clogged up his throat.

Instinctively Dave dropped flat on the compartment catwalk with the extinguisher thrust out in front of him. Yellow smoke now swirled all about him. It was in his mouth, his nose, and in his eyes. It smarted and stung like the pain of a whip lash. He couldn't see. He could only feel. And he felt as though he had suddenly been plunged through the wide open door of a roaring blast furnace. He also felt somebody behind grab his feet and start to drag him backward, but he kicked savagely and got his feet free.

"Don't!" he heard his own voice, which came to him as a faint whisper. "I'm okay. Got to put that out. If it reaches the flare compartment we'll go up like the Fourth of July!"

As he gasped and panted out the words, he worked the fire extinguisher furiously. For a couple of seconds it seemed that he must be pumping the fire-smothering liquid right out a bomber port. The hissing rose to a roar, and puddles of white and blue flame seemed to come sweeping along the catwalk toward Dave. The heat on his face and hands was terrific. The skin all over his body seemed to shrivel up and curl. But he clenched his teeth and pumped harder.

Maybe it was a few seconds, or maybe it was a few years, before the pools of blue-white flame started to fall back and simmer down to a weird glow. That he was gaining on it filled Dave with new strength. He wiggled up onto his knees, sprayed the fire-smothering liquid for all

he was worth, and went creeping forward little
by little. The blue-white flames on the catwalk
died out completely, and Dave raised the nose
of the extinguisher and sprayed the walls on
both sides of the compartment. It was not until
he got to his feet that he realized that Freddy
was at his side pumping away with an extinguisher of his own, and that the Flight Engineer
was right behind them spraying his fire killer
over their shoulders.

And then finally all signs of live flames were
gone. There was nothing but thin choking
smoke, and a whole section of the interior of the
bomber black and charred by flame. The char
marks reached to a point no more than four
inches from the flare lockers, and there they
stopped abruptly. Dave stopped pumping, lowered his extinguisher and reached for one of the
compartment ports to shove it open and let some
of the acrid smoke escape. He missed the port,
however. Things spun furiously for a moment.
When they stopped spinning he was slumped
down on his knees, and Freddy and the Flight
Engineer were bending over him anxiously.

"You all right, Dave?" Freddy asked. "You'd
have cracked your head a fine one, if I hadn't
caught you in time."

"Knew you'd be right there, pal, so I didn't worry," Dave said with a grin and got to his feet. "Boy! That was something while it lasted, huh? Darnedest fire I ever saw."

"Thank God, and you, Dawson, it didn't reach the flare compartment!" the Flight Engineer said fervently. "That would have meant curtains for this baby—and us."

"But that's just like Dawson!" Freddy said proudly. "Always there in the nick of time."

"Nuts!" Dave snorted. "I wasn't thinking of the bomber, or you fellows. I was thinking of just *me,* if you've got to know the truth. But how did the thing get started? What was in that locker?"

"Nothing," the Flight Engineer replied in a puzzled tone.

Something seemed to turn over in Dave's chest. His heart became a little icy, and countless cold shivers went rippling down his spine.

"Nothing?" he echoed, tight-lipped. "You mean—nothing? Nothing at all?"

"Positive of it!" the Flight Engineer replied, and gave him a sharp look. "That locker's for an extra gunner's kit when the bomber is fitted out for active service. I know it was empty because I took a look before we left Seattle yesterday. But stick here. I've got to relieve Major Hawks at the controls so he can come back. And as I said, thank God, and you, Dawson. That was one of the nerviest things I ever saw pulled. Why you aren't burnt to a crisp—!"

The Flight Engineer let the rest go unsaid and, squeezing Dave's arm, stepped past him and hurried forward. For a long minute Dave stood perfectly still, staring down at the smoke and flame marks. Then he looked at Freddy, and there was smouldering rage in his eyes.

"The dirty low-down rat!" he got out viciously. "The—the— Nuts! There aren't the right words in the language to say what I'm thinking right now. He'd not only have finished us off, but probably the skeleton crew aboard this bomber as well."

Freddy returned his gaze and slowly widened his eyes as the full meaning of Dave's words sank home.

"You really think—?" he began, then stopped and began again. "You really think this wasn't an accident?"

"What else?" Dave demanded, and pointed a finger at the locker with the blown off door. "He swears that locker was empty. I believe him. So *you* tell me how an empty locker can explode, blow off its door, and splash that weird-looking blue-white fire all over the place?"

Freddy Farmer stared down at the explosion-damaged locker, too, and shivered slightly.

"Of course, you're right," he muttered. "A time set incendiary bomb, with just enough explosive in it to blow off that door so the flames could spread. Good grief, Dave, if it *had* reached that flare compartment with all those flares—"

The English youth stopped and shuddered violently.

"Yes, it wouldn't have been fun!" Dave said grimly. "It would have been a sweet mess, or worse. We'd—"

Dave cut off the rest. Major Hawks, in command of the ferry bomber, was hurrying aft. The senior officer took a few more steps, then pulled up short and stared wide-eyed at the fire damage. His jaw was set like a chunk of granite, and his eyes glittered like highly polished steel. After a moment or so he glanced up and sought Dave's eyes. The corners of his mouth twitched in a faint grin, and he gave a little nod of his head.

"Lieutenant Kelley says we owe you a vote of thanks, Captain," he said. "And by Jove, we certainly do!"

"That has to include Lieutenant Kelley, and Farmer, too, sir," Dave said. "I'd never have put it out alone. I just happened to see the smoke first, and got first crack at it. As a matter of fact, it was Lieutenant Kelley who attracted my attention by saying he smelled something funny. Personally, I'm thankful he came aft to get some eats ready. If he hadn't, we probably wouldn't have noticed anything until it was too late to do much about it."

The Major grunted, started to say something, but checked himself, and took a step toward the explosion-damaged locker. Sticking out one foot, he toed out a small black object from the floor of the flame-blackened locker. When he bent down to examine it both Dave and Freddy were right there with him. The black object was about two inches long, round, and about as thick as a man's middle finger. It was open at both ends, and it was obviously made of metal.

"What in thunder?" Major Hawks breathed, and tried to touch it with a finger, but found it was too hot. "This looks like a piece of small pipe."

"It is, sir," Freddy Farmer said quietly. "It's one end of a pencil incendiary bomb that wasn't melted by the terrific heat, I fancy."

The bomber's commander snapped his head up sharply.

"Huh, what's that?" he barked. "A pencil incendiary bomb? This?"

"What's left of it, sir," Freddy said with a nod. "They are usually about four or five inches long. It is divided in the center by a copper disc. One kind of eating acid is poured in one end, and sealed with wax. Another kind of acid is poured in the other, and sealed up. The two acids eat into the copper disc in the middle, and when they mingle they explode and give off a terrific heat."

"Oh, yes, I remember about reading of these things in the last war," the Major said absently. "German spies in the States used to toss them into cargos going aboard ship. When the ship got out to sea, it caught on fire."

"That's right, sir," Freddy said. "And the thickness of the copper disc in the middle determined the time the fire would occur."

"Yeah, sure," Major Hawks grunted. Then, stiffening slightly, he barked, "But what's one of these things doing aboard my Fortress? Holy smoke! Sabotage! Sabotage in the air! I'll radio the rest of the flight to go through their ships

with a fine toothed comb. God grant me time!"
This last breathed as a prayer.

Dave opened his mouth to speak, but suddenly thought better of it. He let the Major
whirl around and dash back toward the radio
nook.

"Perhaps it's better to let him go," Freddy
Farmer murmured. "To let him think that, eh?"

Dave didn't answer at once. He stepped over
to one of the ports, and peered out into the surrounding sky. Though he was sure that he
would spot them, nevertheless a great feeling of
relief surged through him when he counted the
five other Flying Fortresses winging along behind in loose formation. Presently he turned
from the port and looked at Freddy, and slowly
closed his hands into rock hard fists. He gave a
vicious nod of his head as he spoke.

"This is the end!" he grated out. "I'm fed up
to the teeth with being a clay pigeon for unseen
sharpshooters."

"What do you mean?" Freddy asked with a
faint trace of anxiety in his voice.

"What I said!" Dave grunted. "First it was
Frisco, then it was Albuquerque, and now it's
practically Brownsville. Well, that's enough of
that business for me. Now we'll give those rats

something to *really* think about!"

"Oh, quite!" Freddy echoed, tight-lipped. "Quite. But would you mind telling me just what's in your mind? Or is it too great a secret?"

"Keep your shirt on, and come back to earth!" Dave snapped at him. "It's no secret between you and me. When we get to Brownsville, we're borrowing a plane and we're going back to Albuquerque!"

The English born air ace couldn't speak for a moment. He could only stare at Dawson in dumbfounded amazement.

"Going back to Albuquerque?" he finally managed to choke out. "Are you mad?"

"I'm plenty mad!" Dave told him. "But not the way you're thinking, pal. Just relax and leave everything to me. I've got an idea, I have. Just follow my lead, and maybe everything will turn out swell."

"Which, of course, means not to question you, eh?" Freddy murmured. "Right-o, then. I don't see why I agree with you so often, but I do. I suppose that means you have one or two good points. Very well, I'll just relax and let you lead the blasted parade."

Dave just looked at him, grinned, and winked.

CHAPTER TWELVE

Lightning Wings

IN DUE TIME the ferry bomber flight circled the Air Base at Brownsville, and then dropped down one by one to land and trundle over to the hangar line to be taken over by the mechanics. The Fortress in which Dave and Freddy were passengers dropped down first. A crowd of officers and mechanics gathered about it instantly, for Major Hawks had radioed ahead. When Dave and Freddy climbed down they were the center of all eyes. It was obvious that Major Hawks had made more than just a cut and dried report.

No sooner were their feet on the ground than Colonel Bates, Commandant of the Base, stepped over to Dawson and saluted smartly.

"Congratulations, and thank you, Captain Dawson," he said, and smiled. "Major Hawks gave me a full report, and—well, the whole Air Corps is grateful. That was a fine display of courage."

"Thank you, sir," Dave replied, blushing a little. "But as I told Major Hawks, my efforts would have been a waste of time if it hadn't been for Lieutenant Kelley and Captain Farmer. They deserve as much praise as I do, and considerably more, I guess."

"Well, it was a darn good job by everyone concerned," the Base Commandant responded. "We surely can't afford to lose a single ship through accident. And, by the way, just what caused the accident, anyway? You didn't say in your radio report."

Colonel Bates turned and spoke the last to Major Hawks, who had climbed down out of the Flying Fortress. The big bomber's commander held out the flame-blackened length of pipe for the Colonel to see.

"This, sir," he said. "Captain Farmer says it's part of a melted pencil incendiary. I think he's right. Looks like somebody didn't want us to arrive here in one piece. I ordered the others to search their ships. They did, but didn't find anything."

"An acid bomb!" Colonel Bates breathed fiercely and bent over to inspect the short length of small pipe in Major Hawks' hands. "Well, by George! What do you know about that? The war right in our laps! I guess they picked on just one ship, Major, so's we'd think it was a short circuit, or something. Why, the black-hearted skunks. I wonder when it was put there?"

"It must have been at Albuquerque, sir," Lieutenant Kelley spoke up. "It wasn't there when we took off from Seattle. And Albuquerque was our next stop."

"Well, I'll make a report to Intelligence about this!" Colonel Bates said grimly. Then, smiling at Dawson, "But I guess you want to clean up a bit, don't you, Captain? Your little adventure sort of mussed up your uniform a bit. And yours, too, Farmer. We'll hunt up something for you to wear while the field cleaners fix up your uniforms. And is there anything else I can do for you, to show how grateful I am for your job?"

"Thanks, sir," Dave said. "Farmer missed his lunch on account of the fire, so I know he's starved. He has six meals a day, sir, you know. Doctor's orders, I think he once said. But, seriously, I guess we all could do with a bite, if it wouldn't be much trouble. And later—later, could Farmer and I have a word with you?"

"All the words you want, Captain," Colonel Bates said lightly, but shot Dave a keen stare. "First, though, a little food all around. And if you can stand a Base Commandant eating with you, I think I'll join the party. It's for all the bomber crews, of course, Major Hawks."

"I accept for all of them, Colonel," Major Hawks said with a laugh. "Even if the others ate en route, it wasn't more than just a light lunch. Thank you very much, sir."

A little over an hour later the ferry bomber crews and their two distinguished passengers had eaten their fill. Inwardly Dave breathed a great sigh of relief when Colonel Bates pushed back his chair and stood up. Not that he hadn't enjoyed eating with the pilots and bomber crews. It was simply that he and Freddy were the two heroes of the day, and the other bomber members made them repeat their stories over and over again. Of course that led to much talk about sabotage, and how the pencil incendiary had gotten in there in the first place? And particularly who could have done it?

Dave didn't have a correct answer to the last, of course. But both Freddy and he certainly knew why. And to sit there and shake their heads and look as puzzled as the next man was the kind of an ordeal they didn't want to go through every day, or every week, or month, for that matter.

Finally, though, Colonel Bates signalled that the meal was at an end by pushing back his chair and standing up. He glanced down the table at Freddy and Dave.

"And, now," he said, "you two want to chat with me? Let's get along to my office. Excuse us, Gentlemen."

Everybody else rose and stood at attention while the Base Commandant led Dave and Freddy out of the mess. He went through the outer door and across one corner of the field toward his office. As he kept step with the senior officer Dave took a quick look at the planes lined up on the field. When he spotted a couple of Vultees a happy smile flitted across his lips. Freddy saw the sudden smile but didn't say anything. He simply gave Dave a half angry frown and walked along.

When they were inside his office, Colonel Bates dropped into his desk chair, and waved a hand at a couple of other chairs.

"Sit down, you two," he said. Then, giving Dave a keen look, he added, "I suppose it's about that pencil incendiary business, isn't it? I've had the feeling there was more you could tell me about it. Well, go ahead, because my curiosity is getting more altitude with every second."

Dave hesitated, looked at Freddy for a moment, and thought he read complete agreement in his pal's eyes.

"Well, there isn't much else we really can tell you, sir," he said. "Except that the thing was unquestionably slipped aboard at Albuquerque. It was, of course, after the bombers had been there awhile, and Farmer and I had been assigned to Major Hawks' plane."

"I see," Colonel Bates said quietly, when Dave paused for breath. "Go on. You have an idea who did it? And of course, you know *why,* don't you?"

"I don't know who, and neither does Farmer, sir," Dave replied. "But we do know why. Frankly, it was to stop us from arriving here. Because of the request I wish to make, sir, I think Farmer and I should admit to you that we are on an Intelligence job. The details, of course, we can't reveal. But—well, things are getting just a bit too hot for comfort, and—"

Dave hesitated and shot a quick side glance at Freddy. But the English youth wasn't looking at him. He was staring at the opposite wall, and his youthful face was a complete blank.

"And what, Dawson?" Colonel Bates encouraged. "Let's have it."

"I would like to borrow one of your Vultees out there for a return flight to Albuquerque," Dave finally said. "If you wish authority for the request, sir, you can radio Colonel Welsh at the Frisco Air Base."

"I don't need to radio Colonel Welsh," Colonel Bates said with a faint smile. "You see—I've already received my orders, while you were in the air on the way down from Albuquerque. Oh, don't look so alarmed, Dawson. My orders were simply to grant any request you put to me. On my honor, I haven't the faintest idea why you are—were on your way to the Canal Zone by ferry bomber. But, well—well, you two have a bit of a reputation, you know."

"Only too well, sir," Dave said with a groan. "Maybe we've served our usefulness in Intelligence work! We don't seem to be recognized any more than Santa Claus would be. Maybe we'd better wear false beards and wigs, or something."

"Oh, I wouldn't say it was as bad as that yet," the Base Commandant said with a laugh. "I wouldn't say that anybody here at the Base connects your arrival here with Intelligence work. It's simply that when I received Colonel

Welsh's code message I put two and two together, and got four. So you want to return to
Albuquerque, huh?"

"Yes, sir," Dave said, and ignored the searching gaze Freddy Farmer was now giving him.
"Not right at this minute, of course. An hour
or two before midnight, tonight, will be plenty
of time. But we do wish to return."

"Naturally your wish must be granted," the
senior officer said, and grinned. "I don't suppose
you could give me a reason, eh? Something
happened en route that gave you ideas about
Albuquerque?"

Dave grinned at him, and nodded.

"Something did happen en route, sir," he
said. "That pencil incendiary fire. And it did
give me ideas. I'm sorry, sir, but that's as far as
I'd care to go."

"Then it'll have to be far enough for me, I
guess," the Base Commandant said with a sigh
of disappointment. "A little before midnight,
eh? Okay, then. The Vultee will be all gassed
and ready for you then. One more question,
though—that is, if you'd care to answer it. Was
this the first attempt made on your lives?"

"It was the third," Dave said quietly. Then
he added, "And I'm hoping there won't be a

fourth before we leave."

Colonel Bates' eyes popped, and he whistled softly.

"The *third?*" he echoed in amazement. "Well, that shows that the third time isn't a sure thing, as the saying goes. And as regards there being a fourth time here at Brownsville—"

The Base Commandant paused. A thin smile touched his lips, but his eyes were as hard and cold as chiseled ice.

"Then they'll get me, too," he said presently, "whoever they are, because I'm not going to leave you two for an instant until you're off the ground and in the air, and on your way north."

"Thanks for the protection, sir," Dave said with a short laugh. "But I don't look for, or expect any trouble here. I think our rat friends were counting on that bomber fire being a sure thing."

"Quite." Freddy Farmer nodded for emphasis. "Good grief, how close it came to being just that! Every time I see a flare locker after this I'm sure I'll break out in a sweat. But I agree with Dave, sir. I don't think we'll have any trouble here. I certainly hope not."

The Base Commandant chuckled and made a little gesture.

"Well, it's been pretty dead around here," he said almost wistfully. "I think we could do with a little excitement, provided, of course, that nobody on our side gets hurt. But just the same, I'm going to stick close to you two. How about a look around the field as a starter? We've got some pretty interesting stuff here."

"I'd like that very much, sir," Dave said eagerly. "I saw that you have quite a few of the new types."

"Yes," Freddy echoed, his face brightening. "I'd jolly well like to look around a bit."

"Then what are we waiting for?" Colonel Bates grinned, and got to his feet. "Let's go!"

Then began a most pleasant afternoon for the two young air aces. They saw everything there was to see at the Brownsville Base, and it was all so terribly interesting that they almost forgot the ever present mystery menace that hung over them like a dark cloud. But not quite. Every so often, in a flash of memory, stark reality would return to one or the other of them, and they would have to try hard not to let it show in their faces.

Just before evening mess the six ferry bombers took off on the last lap of their journey to the bomber base in the Canal Zone. Freddy watched them with a faint sadness in his eyes, and a sort of empty, hollow feeling inside of him. He constantly shot sneak side glances at Dave, but there was nothing but a grin and a contented look on Dawson's face. Each time Freddy would switch his gaze away, frown, and bite at his lower lip. Could it be that Dave—? Not once would he let himself finish the thought. It most certainly wasn't a question of courage with Dave—that he was getting the wind up after so many escapes from death, and in such rapid succession. It was something else, and Freddy wished to high Heaven that Dave would please break down and let him in on his secret—if there was a secret

When the last of the ferry bombers had lost itself in the growing dusk far to the south, Freddy half turned toward Dave, but didn't look at him.

"Don't you wish we were aboard one of those?" he murmured so nobody else could hear, "heading down toward the Canal Zone to learn what we can from Second Lieutenant Marble?"

Dave looked at him, and shrugged.

"Aboard one of those?" he echoed. "Nix! Once is enough for me. Too darn dangerous. Well, let's go eat."

Freddy Farmer's jaw dropped, and a hurt look flooded into his eyes.

"Dave!" he began, and couldn't go on.

Dawson just grinned at him, and then suddenly winked.

"Remember your stomach, little boy," he chuckled a moment later. "It's a long ride back to Albuquerque. Let's go fill it up."

At mess there was a lot of general talk, but very little of it came from Colonel Bates' lips. Dave caught him glancing his way several times, and there was a look of puzzled disapproval in the Base Commandant's eyes. Dave had a pretty fair hunch that the Colonel had heard him make that crack to Freddy about it being too darn dangerous in bombers. Oh well, it didn't matter what anybody thought. Yet, on the contrary, it mattered a lot. Yes! Just so long as they thought the things he hoped they would think.

Eventually the time for Dave and Freddy to take off rolled around. Colonel Bates and a couple of the other officers walked out with them to where the Vultee was waiting. But when Dave reached it he didn't climb up into the pit. Instead he walked deliberately to the *next* Vultee in line, and climbed aboard it.

Colonel Bates stopped dead in his tracks, and gaped.

"But this is your plane, Dawson," he said, and pointed to the first Vultee.

"I know, sir," Dave said easily, and motioned to Freddy to leg in back. "But I suddenly want to take this one. It's all right, isn't it, sir?"

The Base Commandant gulped, looked angry for a moment, and then shrugged.

"I guess it is," he said. "They're both all set for flight. Yes, go ahead and take it, if it makes you feel any better."

"It does, and thanks, sir," Dave said, and jabbed the starter button. After he got the Wright Cyclone kicking over, and throttled down to warm up revs, he looked at the Base Commandant and smiled again. "Thanks for everything, sir!" he called out. "Is there anything I can do at Albuquerque for you?"

"Nothing that I can think of," Colonel Bates replied dryly. "Just tell them we can handle all the ferry planes they send along. And we hope they'll send along a lot."

"I'll tell them that, sir," Dave said. Then, twisting around in the pit, he called out, "All set, Freddy? All strapped in, and got your hot water bottle handy?"

"Quite!" the English youth replied in a flat tone. "And I don't think *I* need a hot water bottle!"

Dave kept the grin on his face, but there was suddenly a tiny ache in his heart. That last from Freddy had hit just a trifle below the belt. Guess Freddy was getting ideas that maybe he was losing his grip. Well—what else should he think? Dave shook such thoughts from his head, and reached for the throttle.

"All aboard for Albuquerque!" he shouted, and raised a hand to his helmet in salute to Colonel Bates and his officers. "Thanks again for everything, and I hope we come through here again some day."

Without waiting to see if his salute was returned, or to give anybody a chance to say anything, Dave eased the throttle open and sent the Vultee rolling out to the head end of the lighted runway. He swung around into the wind, got the green light from the signal tower, and fed the Cyclone all the high test hop she could take. As though it were something human, and desperately eager to get into the air, the Vultee streaked forward and picked up more and more speed with every revolution of its steel-bladed prop. Presently Dave lifted it clear, got the wheels up, and the nose pointed toward the crystal-dotted night sky over Texas. He kept on going up until he was a good seventeen thousand above the earth. Then he leveled off and put the plane on a crow flight course for Albuquerque.

He relaxed a bit in the seat, letting the ship fly herself, and sort of waited for words to come from Freddy Farmer's lips. But the English born air ace said nothing. He sat slumped down in his seat, staring at the vast array of twinkling stars overhead. Dave shrugged, grinned in the glow of his instrument panel light, and let the plane fly onward toward Albuquerque.

That is, he flew toward Albuquerque for about ten minutes; then he touched the stick and rudder pedal and veered way around until the Vultee was heading due east. For a second Freddy Farmer didn't notice the abrupt change of course. But when he did he sat up straight, leaned forward a bit and rapped Dave on the shoulder.

"Do you know you're ninety degrees off your course?" he called out.

"No I'm not!" Dave called back, only half turning his head. "I'm right on it, pal. Right on the old beam!"

"Heading due east?" Freddy cried. "Just

where in the world do you think Albuquerque is? Out in the Gulf of Mexico?"

"Albuquerque?" Dave echoed, thoroughly enjoying himself. "Who the thunder said anything about Albuquerque? I didn't have any ideas about going to Albuquerque!"

Dave waited for what he fully expected. And he wasn't disappointed. Suddenly both of Freddy's hands were about his neck, and there was just a suggestion of pressure in the English youth's fingers.

"Blast you, you blighter!" Freddy grated. "And you had us all thinking— You really mean—"

"What else?" Dave chuckled, and lightly knocked Freddy's hands away. "Not that I don't trust you, pal. I just thought it would be a good idea not to say anything to anybody. Albuquerque? Nuts! This train is an express for the Canal Zone. We're due in in about eight hours. So lean back and enjoy yourself, apart from your navigation duties, of course. We've got plenty of gas to make it, but we're not overflowing with it, so don't kick your calculations around. You'll find charts, and stuff, in that side pocket. I slipped them in there just after mess. I don't think the Colonel will miss them. Not sore any more, are you, sweetheart?"

"I should be, but I'm not," Freddy growled. "But I see your point. I guess it was the best idea to say nothing to no one. But why couldn't we have gone by bomber, just the same?"

"Freddy, Freddy!" Dave groaned at him. "And you're attached to Intelligence? I think I'm a little ashamed of you, my boy. Put on your thinking cap, and use some of that stuff you've got in that thick head of yours."

"I already have!" Freddy replied with a faint laugh. "And I'm embarrassed for myself, no end. Of course! It was to throw everybody off the trail, eh? Particularly our rat friends?"

"Check," Dave replied. "There seem to be too many of them, at too many different places. Maybe there wasn't one of them at Brownsville. But there was no way for us to tell for sure. So the best thing to do was to play it safe, to get the word spread around that we were going back to Albuquerque."

"And a double reason, that," Freddy spoke up. "It will not only throw our unknown and unseen friends off the trail, but, no doubt, it will make them wonder just a bit if we have suddenly learned something quite definite about those goings on at Albuquerque."

"That's just the idea!" Dave said with a laugh. "Just one bright little guy, me, huh?"

"On occasion," Freddy snapped. "Only on occasion. But I suppose you realized that our rat friends aren't the only ones you're going to upset?"

"I know," Dave replied gravely. "But nothing can be done about it. When we don't show up at Albuquerque there'll be a lot of planes out looking for our crash. Hate to have all that gas and oil wasted. But our job is to get to the Canal Zone, and get there in shape to start swinging at this confounded mystery with both fists. Gosh! I sure hope and pray it doesn't turn out that we might just as well have gone back to Albuquerque."

"Perish the thought!" Freddy Farmer groaned. "Don't even think of it. But you can start bearing south now. We're well east of Brownsville, and they can't hear our engine. Canal Zone! Here we come, and jolly well keen to make the best of things, and win through in pukka style."

"And you can say that again!" Dave breathed fervently, and banked the Vultee around until it was headed south and slipping out over the night-darkened waters of the Gulf of Mexico.

CHAPTER THIRTEEN

Invisible Fate

THE NEW SUN had been up for a couple of hours and its pure golden rays played tag on the wings of the Vultee as the two seater attack craft droned steadily onward. Long ago Dave had tired of watching the deep blue Caribbean roll by beneath him. He had also tired of spotting the little groups of cays that stuck up out of the water here and there. An hour ago they had skirted the most eastern tip of Nicaragua, and now they were thundering straight down the world toward Panama. An hour at the most and they would be sliding down to a landing on the Air Corps Base at Colon, on the Caribbean side of the Canal.

An hour at the most. Dave sighed, pushed up his goggles and dug knuckles into his tired eyes. It had been a pretty monotonous trip. Just drilling along in the dark of night well off shore of the Central American countries, so that they wouldn't be mistaken for enemy aircraft and get a few anti-aircraft shells tossed up at them. Just drilling along with nothing to break up the flight and make it more interesting. Of course, in his heart that was the last thing Dave wanted. Or Freddy Farmer, either, for that matter. Still, it was nice to imagine that it would help a little if a Messerschmitt or two should come streaking out of nowhere with all guns blazing. Nothing so soul-satisfying as smacking a couple of Nazis before breakfast.

Dave pulled the string on his crazy, rambling thoughts, and shifted his position in the seat.

"You still there, Freddy?" he called out. "Or was that air bump a ways back you jumping out?"

"It wasn't," Freddy replied. "But I'll admit I've been toying with the thought. Too bad this isn't a seaplane. Then we could at least land down there and have a swim."

"And maybe a shark or two for company?" Dave laughed. "No thanks, pal. Those things can go a whole lot faster than I can. When it comes to swimming down there, I like it fine up here. Well, say something! Keep the conversation going before I fall asleep, and we *do* land down there—in a heap."

"Keep the conversation going yourself!" Freddy growled back at him. "I'm quite content just to listen to the sound of your voice. Though, of course, I've heard much better voices, not so much like pebbles rattling around in a tin can."

"Bum!" Dave snorted. "For that I should keep my trap shut and let you go quietly screwy by yourself. But seeing it's you, I won't. What do you know about the Panama Canal, Freddy?"

"A fair amount, I fancy," the English youth replied. "I studied geography in school, you know."

"Oh!" Dave echoed. "Then you *did* go to school? I've often wondered. Fine, then. Tell me this, student. Supposing you entered the Canal at the Colon end? Where would you be headed?"

"For the Pacific," was the instant reply. "Or, to be exact, for the Bay of Panama."

"Nuts to you!" Dave barked. "I mean, what direction?"

"What direction?" Freddy echoed. "The bloke must be mad, and completely off his topper. Why, west, of course!"

Dave twisted around in the seat and made a face.

"See?" he cried. "No brains, as I've always said. Or at least, what goes in there doesn't stay for long. Stand in the corner for a while, my little man. Then take a good look at those map charts of yours back there."

"Eh, what?" Freddy grunted.

"What I said," Dave replied. "Take a gander at those map charts back there. Then come around front, here, and beg me to let you remain in the classroom."

"Rot!" Freddy muttered. "You're talking crazy rubbish, and I fancy—"

The English youth's voice trailed off, and it became obvious that he was studying his map charts of the Canal and surrounding area. Dave took a quick look back to make sure, then turned front and waited for the explosion. It came at the end of perhaps twenty-five seconds.

"Good grief!" the words burst forth from the English youth's lips. "Why—why, I always thought—!"

"You, and a few million other people!" Dave said with a laugh as Freddy stumbled. "The Panama Canal does *not* run from east to west. It's from west to east. Or if you want to get technical about it, the Canal runs from the northwest to the southeast. It's the cockeyed bend in the Republic of Panama that makes it that way. Remember that little item, Freddy. It may help you to be the life of the party some day."

"Thank you, no!" the English youth grunted. "But that certainly is amazing! I mean, it's certainly something new I've learned."

"Stick around," Dave chuckled. "I'll get you educated, if it kills me. But pass over one of those charts, will you? One you're not using. I want to have a look at it myself."

Freddy Farmer did as he was asked. Dave took the chart tacked to the board, rested it against the top of the joy stick and began to study it. Perhaps two minutes later a white light seemed to explode in his head. He let out a wild yell, lurched in the seat, and unconsciously sent the Vultee nosing down into a crazy power dive. Freddy Farmer's voice in his ears was a scream.

"Dave, good grief! What's happened? Are you all right? What's the matter?"

Dave's eyes were bulging out, and his heart was hammering furiously against his ribs as he recovered from the sudden dive and brought the Vultee back onto even keel.

"I knew it, I *knew* it!" he choked out.

"Knew what?" Freddy cried angrily. "For Heaven's sake, what's got into you?"

"Another hunk of the mystery puzzle, Freddy!" Dave shouted as he twisted around in the seat. "Remember how I said we should both keep chewing over poor Tracey's four words that sounded like Albuquerque? Well, that's just what he meant, Freddy. But *not* Albuquerque, New Mexico!"

"No?" the English youth cried breathlessly, and leaned way forward so that he could see the map chart Dave Dawson held in his hands. "Then what did he mean?"

"He said 'southern Albuquerque*s*'!" Dave cried. "Get it? *Plural!* That's what he meant—*right there!*"

As Dave spoke the last he touched a fingertip to a point on the map chart. It was a group of tiny islands about a hundred and twenty-five miles due east of the central east coast of Nicaragua. And right underneath the group of tiny dots was printed:

ALBUQUERQUE CAYS

Freddy had been holding his breath while he stared at the map chart, and when he let it out it was close to the whistle of a locomotive.

"Good grief, you're right, of course, Dave!" he cried. "If he mentioned the words 'Cays,' we must have missed it completely. But I'll swear I didn't hear any word that sounded like cays, did you?"

"No, he didn't speak it," Dave replied with a vigorous shake of his head. "He just said 'southern Albuquerques.' And I'll eat my shirt if those southernmost cays there aren't what he was trying to get over to us."

"I don't think you'll have to have that kind of a meal," the English youth said with a grin. "I'm sure you're right. But what about it? Those cays are quite a bit in back of us now. Think we should turn around and have a look?"

Dave glanced at the fuel gauges before he replied. He shook his head.

"No, I don't think we'd better, Freddy," he said. "It would mean shaving our gas supply too close for comfort. Now that we feel sure we've got our teeth into something, the last thing we want to do is sit down in the middle of the Caribbean. Nope! I think our best bet is to carry on to Colon and contact Second Lieutenant Marble. There's just a chance he might give us a whole lot of dope on this. He— Now what's the matter?"

Freddy was scowling out across the air space and absently shaking his head.

"Nothing, probably," he said eventually. "But about this Marble—I'm afraid I have a very definite opinion about him, Dave. Call it a hunch, if you like."

"I like," Dave grunted. "So what's the hunch? Tell me."

"That Second Lieutenant Marble is going to turn out an awful big disappointment to us," the English youth said. "I can't suppress the feeling that we won't learn a single thing from him. Why I feel this way, I haven't the faintest idea. But I do, just the same."

"Well, now that we're letting down our hair, I might as well admit that I'm clamping down on my own hopes," Dave said. "I figure it this way. If Marble was working hand in glove with Tracey on this business, I think Marble would have been sent north to contact Colonel Welsh, and not Tracey. If the thing was red hot, I can't see him leaving the scene of action. But—but, darn it, maybe I'm just talking through my hat. Maybe this Tracey business and the southern Albuquerque Cays doesn't add up to a single thing of importance."

"Maybe it doesn't," Freddy grunted with a shrug. "Just the same, I think I'd be willing to bet my life that it does. Blast it, Dave! Too many attempts to wash us out were made, not to have this thing be at white heat."

"Yes," Dave said with a nod. "You've got

something there, pal. You definitely have. Well, we shall see what we shall see. Right now we're getting close to the edge of the air patrol area of the Canal Zone. We should be bumping into Army or Navy planes most any minute now."

"Well, see that you don't *actually* bump into them," Freddy added grimly, and settled back in his seat.

It was just exactly eleven minutes later when two U. S. Naval Aviation patrol amphibians came into Dave's range of vision. He raised his hand to attract Freddy's attention and then pointed at the two craft off the left wing and a few miles ahead.

"Yes, I saw them," the English youth called out. "And as we're arriving down here unannounced, I hope those blighters don't do anything serious about it. I hope they don't take us for a couple of Jap spies on our way to take pictures of the Canal."

"If they do, I'll never forgive them!" Dave said with a laugh.

Just the same his eyes narrowed slightly as the two amphibians broke wing tip formation and sheered away from each other so that they would come up on the Vultee, one on either side. And his heart wasn't exactly beating peace-

fully in his breast, either. In fact, for a fleeting
instant he wondered whether he had been wise
to make this sneak flight down to the Canal
Zone. Right! There was a very good chance that
maybe the gunners aboard those patrolling amphibians might have itching trigger fingers.

So he decided to do something about it first.
He banked the Vultee sharply so that he pre-
sented a broadside view to the oncoming amphibians, and also showed his Brownsville Base
markings. Then he cut around back to present
the other side, and stuck his hand up through
his opened greenhouse and waved it in greeting.

Then followed a few anxious moments. The
two amphibians came plowing onward. They
swept past the Vultee one on each side, and
Dave could almost feel the pairs of eyes aboard
them boring out at him. He waved his hand
again, and then throttled to give the two Navy
aircraft plenty of time to bank around and come
up on him from the rear.

"Unsociable blighters, aren't they!" Freddy
Farmer grunted. "Not a return wave of greeting from either of them."

"You can't blame them," Dave defended
them. "They're on a job that doesn't call for any
kidding around. They have to play it close, and

not stick their necks out. But I guess we've passed muster. They're just going to ride herd on us the rest of the way to the Base."

"Oh, quite!" Freddy growled. "And their guns aren't pointed at the sun, either. Gives a chap a creepy feeling, as though he weren't to be trusted."

"There goes your conscience again!" Dawson laughed. "It's your past coming up to slap you in the face, my boy. But don't worry! They'll wait until they get a good look at you on the ground, before they do anything drastic. Of course, when they do—well, it's your face. But I'll put in all the good words I can."

"I just bet you would!" the English youth snapped. "Just enough to get me shot at sunrise. And—I say! There's the Canal. My word! Isn't that a wonderful sight? You can see both oceans at the same time."

"Just the way Nature and Old Father Time arranged it so you could," Dave murmured, and feasted his eyes on one of the most fascinating and thrilling air views in all the world: the Colon entrance of the Panama Canal, and the rest of the Canal clear across the Isthmus to the Balboa entrance on the Pacific side.

Some ten or fifteen minutes later he eased

back the Vultee's throttle and sent the plane sliding down to a landing on the surface of the huge Air Corps Base at Colon. The two amphibians circled about until his wheels had touched, and then they veered off out over the Caribbean to resume their watchful patrol. Freddy Farmer watched them go, and made a face.

"Thanks awfully for the company!" he growled as Dave taxied over toward the check-in office. "Delightful chaps, all of you."

"Right!" Dave barked back at him. "Also, great guys with plenty of what it takes. Give me trouble and I'll welcome help from Navy Aviation boys any day in the week. And so would you!"

"Of course; sorry," Freddy said with a sheepish grin. "I just feel a bit touchy today. After all, I've been subjected to your flying for hours, you know. A frightful ordeal for even the most stout-hearted."

"Coward!" Dave jeered at him. "You wouldn't have dared say that when we were in the air, would you? But it is nice to get back on solid ground again. Sweet tripe! Look at the planes they've got down here! All types from everything to everything, what I mean. Well, get your papers ready, Freddy. They'll want to know who we are, and why."

That fact was indeed true. When Dave finally cut his engine and climbed down to stretch his stiffened legs, there was a questioning-eyed group of Air Corps high rankers gathered in front of the check-in office. Dave waited for Freddy and then walked over and saluted the highest rank smartly. He was a Brigadier General, and, of course, Dave knew that his name was Kirwood.

"Captains Dawson and Farmer, arriving from Brownsville Base, sir," Dave said. "Here are our identification papers."

"Glad to welcome you, Captains Dawson and Farmer," the Brigadier said, though there was a distinct lack of warmth in his voice. "I was informed of your coming yesterday. I thought it was to be by ferry bomber, though. The bombers landed at France Field hours ago."

"We stayed over in Brownsville, sir," Dave explained truthfully. "Borrowed the Vultee."

"I see," the senior officer grunted, and took a moment out to examine the papers the two air aces handed him. When he glanced up there was a slightly brittle look in his eyes. "Down here on an inspection for Washington H. Q., eh?" he said pointedly. "Well, Gentlemen, I hope you'll find everything in order."

"I'm afraid you misunderstand, sir," Dave said with a disarming smile. "But I'll admit it's not stated clearly in our papers. It's not exactly an inspection trip, sir. A survey study, rather. There are plans of making some changes in the attack bomber school of instruction. Frankly, it's our job to pick up all the pointers we can down here with active service squadrons, and make our report direct to Washington. We are simply seeking to learn a few things, sir."

The Brigadier General's suspicious stiffness floated away from his face. He seemed greatly relieved when he smiled.

"Well, I'll admit that's better," he said. "I was afraid that you were just two more Staff officers to get in our hair, and then return to Washington with all kinds of darn fool ideas and suggestions."

"Well, frankly, sir," Dave said with a laugh, "if we were we wouldn't be here. Both Farmer and myself would have chosen the guard house rather than an assignment like that. We—something the matter, sir?"

The last was caused by the Base Commandant staring hard at Dave's tunic and then at

Freddy's. Presently he shook his head, and smiled.

"No, not a thing, Captain Dawson," he said. "I just happened to notice that you both wear the decoration ribbon of the Distinguished Flying Cross. You saw service in the Royal Air Force?" *

"Yes, sir," Dawson replied. "But of course, that was before Pearl Harbor. Well, it's good to be down here, sir. I hope you won't treat us any differently than you would any two replacements. After all, the main job for all of us is to win the war."

"Don't worry," the General chuckled. "I don't plan to extend you two any special privileges, though, of course, you are at liberty to come and go as you please."

"I say, thanks very much, sir," Freddy Farmer spoke up for the first time. Then, after a long moment's hesitation, he suddenly blurted out, "I believe, sir, there's a chap here I know. He is Second Lieutenant Marble. Does he happen to be about?"

A dark shadow passed across Brigadier General Kirwood's face. A hard, bitter look came into his eyes, and he unconsciously

* *"Dave Dawson with the R.A.F."*

clenched both his fists.

"He was, but no longer," the senior officer said harshly. "Two days ago he took off on a check flight alone. Something haywire with his engine, I believe it was. We haven't seen hide nor hair of him since. I am afraid he crashed into the water out there, and sank with his plane."

"Oh, I'm sorry, sir!" Dave murmured as the blood seemed to drain right down out of his body. "I knew Marble slightly, myself. I'm sorry to hear that he is missing. But—well, maybe he force landed some place and will turn up alive and kicking in a day or so."

"I sincerely hope that's true," the Brigadier said gravely. "But I doubt it. Marble is the eighth pilot we've lost on solo flights in the last month. It's—it's the most confounded thing I've ever come up against. I can't understand it."

Neither Dave nor Freddy said anything. They simply looked at each other silently. But the thought in their minds was identical. The most promising clue of all had been snatched from their grasp. It was a worthy foe that they battled, even though a dastardly one. A clever, cunning, ruthless foe who always seemed to strike first, and strike where it hurt the most.

CHAPTER FOURTEEN

Satan's Signals

EXACTLY THIRTY-SIX hours had passed since the arrival of Dave Dawson and Freddy Farmer at the Air Corps Base at Colon in the Canal Zone. Thirty-six hours, during every minute of which they both yearned and longed for decisive action, or at least action of some kind. However, they had parts to play, and they played them for all they were worth. As two special pilots from Washington G.H.Q. they stepped right into the war activities of the Attack Squadron. They attended brush up classes, they took part in the many patrol conferences held in the field's Ready-Room, and they went out and flew formation look-see patrols that carried them far out over the Caribbean, and to the north and south of the Canal Zone.

In short, they did everything to make it look as though they really were down there to learn, and report their knowledge later to Washington. But it was simply a part they were playing, and on the morning of their third day with the Attack Squadron they just couldn't wait any longer. They were on the field, dressed for flying, and watching the routine dawn patrol take off, when Dave mentioned the thought that was ever constant and uppermost in their minds.

"We've got just one more card to play, Freddy," he said in a low voice that didn't carry beyond the ears for which it was meant. "I think we should play it. Take a chance, anyway, and try to find out if we're right or wrong. I'll go plain, raving nuts if we put it off any longer. What do you say?"

"I say, absolutely!" the English youth replied instantly. "One more day and I, too, will be fit for a padded cell, or something. What rotten luck! I mean, Marble being missing."

"And how!" Dave grated softly, and stared up at the cloud-streaked Panama sky. "But pick up first prize. It's yours, Freddy. You certainly called it right on Marble. We sure won't learn a thing from him, because he isn't here. But, gosh! I'm almost afraid to start out."

"The southern Albuquerque Cays, you mean?" Freddy asked, and stared at him wide-eyed. "Why?"

Dave shrugged and gave a little shake of his head.

"Like going down to the post office to find out

if the all important letter you hope is there *is* there," he said after a moment or two. "I mean, if the southern Albuquerque Cays turn out to be just a bust, then where are we? Right behind the old eight ball, and a complete wash-out to Colonel Welsh. Darn it, Freddy, I can take a licking with the best of them, and come up grinning—I hope. But if I fall down on this job I think I'll just walk into the ocean and keep going."

"I know just how you feel, Dave," Freddy said, and sighed heavily. "The fact that we haven't made any headway to speak of in this blasted mess makes it all the more important to us. But, good grief! We had so blasted little to start with in the first place. Of course I'm not complaining, nor trying to make excuses. Just the same, I think this is the first Intelligence job we've tackled where we absolutely bumped head on into a brick wall."

"You've got something there, pal!" Dave grunted. "It's been like shadow boxing, and trying to knock your shadow cold. You start a haymaker up from the floor, and suddenly your shadow isn't there any more. Oh well, we're not going to find out a thing just standing around here gabbing. That's a cinch. Put on your bib and tucker, Freddy. We're going to do a little sky cruising, and see what there is to see. And you know what I'm hoping, I guess?"

"Quite," Freddy breathed softly, and tightened the chin strap of his helmet. "Right-o. Let's get on with the blasted business. If we don't find a thing, we can at least dive straight into the water, and make an end of our troubles."

"And that's an idea, *if!*" Dave grunted, and climbed up into the forward cockpit of the Vultee attack plane. "All aboard!"

A few moments later Dave took the Vultee off, got himself a bit of altitude, then started circling the field to create the impression to any watching eyes below that he and Freddy were just taking a breather hop, and checking their plane. Eventually he let the plane slide away from the Air Base, and guided it out over the reaches of the Caribbean Sea. Presently he spotted the dawn patrol ahead and a little to the south of his position. He climbed the Vultee to high altitude and brought it around and put it on a course that led toward the Albuquerque Cays. They were some two hundred and thirty miles away, and so it was lacking a few minutes of an hour when he finally sighted them ahead and low down on the horizon.

Sight of them made little shivers start rippling up and down his spine. His heart began to hammer, and his mouth and lips went slightly dry. For a moment he was filled with the insane and utterly ridiculous desire to bank around and fly away in the opposite direction. Fear that this last hope would fall through took charge of his nerves, and tiny beads of sweat began to break out on his forehead. He shook his head in an angry gesture and took a tighter hold on the control stick, as though in so doing he could prevent that other half of him from turning the plane away.

"Come on, stop being a silly dope!" he grated at himself. "You're worse than a fellow with his first date with the beautiful girl who just recently moved into the neighborhood. Snap out of it, kid! What is to be, will be. And if it isn't —then, so help me, it'll be up to you to do something about it!"

"Do something about what, Dave?" he heard Freddy Farmer call to him.

He turned around and grinned at his English born pal.

"Just giving myself the old pep talk, Freddy," he said. "Just promising myself that everything's going to turn out okay. And how are all your friends?"

"I've known happier and more contented moments," Freddy replied. Then, lifting a hand and pointing a finger forward, "Well, there they are, old thing, for what they're worth. Better lose some of our altitude so's we can take a good look around. These patches of cloud aren't made of glass, you know."

Dave nodded, turned forward, and throttled the Vultee's Cyclone and let the plane nose down toward the expanse of deep blue Caribbean sea below. When he was at around five thousand feet he leveled off and headed straight for the Albuquerque Cays. Coming up on them, they looked like lush green and brown dots on a field of blue. And when he was directly over the first dot of the short curving chain of islands they didn't look like very much more. He counted six of them, the biggest being the most northern one. But nowhere did he see any signs of life. For all you could tell a subterranean volcanic disturbance might possibly have pushed them up above the surface of the water overnight. Just patches of green and brown on a field of blue. Patches of green and brown that were edged here and there by strips of yellowish white, that were actually beaches.

For a good half hour Dave drilled up and down over the Albuquerque Cays searching every square inch of them with his eyes. However, as each second clicked away into the history of time, his heart sank lower and lower, and the flame of hope in him grew smaller and smaller. He didn't dare turn around and look at Freddy, for he knew that he would only see his own misery reflected in his pal's eyes. So he kept his face front and continued to circle about over the Cay chain. More time passed, and the hope in him died down to a tiny spark.

Throttling the Wright-powered Vultee V-12C attack bomber to cruising speed, Dave licked his dry lips, twisted around in the seat, and winked at Freddy Farmer in the gunner's pit.

"How's it go, pal?" he called out, and motioned downward. "Not nervous, or anything like that, are you?"

"Certainly not!" the English boy shouted back. "I stopped being nervous hours ago. Now I'm simply *scared stiff* that we're wrong! How do you feel?"

Dave shrugged and made a little gesture with his free hand.

"I'm not sure," he said, "but I guess it's something like the way a clay pigeon must feel. You know, hoping the guy with the trap gun will miss. But—but I'm afraid this is a waste of time, and that we've struck out."

"Not any more!" Freddy shouted, and pointed to the left. "Look! Do you see it? Recognize the type?"

Dave instantly turned his head to face east, and peered hard at the cloud-dotted blue sky. For a second or so he didn't see a thing but clouds and blue sky. Then suddenly he saw a dot moving along the underneath side of one of the clouds. But it was just a moving dot to him. A plane, of course. But as far as he was concerned, it could well be a free balloon at that distance. He looked back again at Freddy and was startled by the wildly excited look on his pal's face.

"Recognize the type?" he echoed. "What do you think I've got here? An X-ray machine for distance. And what's eating you? What's making you so excited, for cat's sake?"

"Who wouldn't be?" the English youth yelled back at him, and stabbed the air with his pointed finger. "You should get some glasses. Dave, that plane up there is one of the new

Nazi Arados! The folding wing type that they can carry aboard the larger type of German U-boats. You know, they use them for scouting convoys and stragglers left behind. That's what that is up there—one of the new Nazi Arados! I could spot one of those in the dark. So I know I'm absolutely right!"

Dave's mouth fell open in dumbfounded amazement, and for a second or two he couldn't move, much less speak a word.

"What?" he finally bellowed. "A Nazi U-boat plane? You're sure?"

"Yes!" Freddy barked at him. "Yes, for goodness' sake, let's do something about it before the blighter sees *us*, and hides away in one of those clouds."

Long before Freddy Farmer had finished his words, Dave had whirled around front and was feeding the thundering Wright Cyclone every ounce of high test octane it could take. He hauled the Vultee around and stuck the nose up toward the clouds in the distance. He leaned forward against the controls and strained his eyes upward. It wasn't until a few seconds had ticked by that he really got a good look at the plane's silhouette stamped on a background cloud. But when he did get that good look, there was no longer the slightest doubt that Freddy had been seeing things.

It was a Nazi U-boat Arado, right enough. He could see the biplane wings, the rounded fuselage with the radial engine in the nose, and the war painted pontoon fitted underneath. He stared at it for several moments as the Vultee went prop screaming upwards. Then he impulsively lowered his gaze and swept the stretches of the Caribbean below him. But to his disappointment he didn't see any U-boat on the surface of the water, or below it, for that matter. Nor was there any telltale thread-like wake of a periscope going through the water. There was nothing but just blue water, and not the sign of a single vessel of any description.

"More speed, Dave!" came Freddy's excited cry to his ears. "I think the beggar has seen us. Yes, he has! And there he goes for that big cloud. Blast it! If only he were in range!"

Dave made no comment. His eyes were again on the tiny Nazi seaplane, and he could see it scooting upward toward the white fluffy belly of a great big cloud.

"Let him hide in it!" he presently growled. "We'll go in after him and smoke him out. Get those rear guns ready, Freddy!"

"Think I'd forgotten them!" the English youth snapped. "You just get us up there. That's all you have to worry about!"

Dave had to grin in spite of himself. Good old Freddy Farmer! As meek as a mouse when nothing special was happening. But let action show up and at the drop of a hat he was like a snarling tiger.

"If we don't find him," Dave grunted as he saw the tiny Arado slide up into the cloud and disappear, "I'll probably have my hands full stopping Freddy from getting out and looking around. Well, here we go in after him. And if we smack into him, it's going to be his job that'll break up like toothpicks, not this tough Vultee."

As Dave spoke the last he lifted the nose a bit more and then went slashing up into the cloud. In nothing flat he was tearing through a glistening white world that seemingly tried to crowd right down into the cockpit. Hand steady on the stick, and body bent well forward, he peered hard into the glistening mist, ready at an instant's notice to fire his forward guns and swerve off sharply if the shadow of the other plane should suddenly loom up in front of his propeller.

However, no shadow loomed up before him,

nothing but white mist that glistened in the blazing rays of the tropical sun. And then, suddenly, the Vultee went ripping up out of the cloud and into clear air. No sooner was he out in the open than Dave leveled off from his zoom, and twisted around and stared down back at the top of the cloud. It seemed almost to wink at him mockingly. There was no sign of hide nor hair of the Arado.

"Lost him, blast it!" Freddy Farmer grated.

"Keep your shirt on!" Dave snapped. "We'll find him. He can't be far. Just take it easy, and be ready to smack him when he comes up through."

"*If* he does!" the English youth groaned, and then fell silent.

Dave didn't say anything, either. He simply tooled the Vultee back and forth over the cloud and kept his eyes riveted on its fluffy crest. Presently he slid down through it again to clear air below. In fact, he practically combed the cloud with the Vultee, but that was all the good it did him.

"Well, that's a horse on me, Freddy," he was eventually forced to admit sadly. "Sorry, Freddy. I guess he put one over on me and sneaked over to some other of these clouds. The darned plane is so small you could hide it under your hat."

"Anyway, the venture had a promise of excitement," Freddy grunted. "What now? I don't think there's any sense hunting around for the blighter. We could run out of gas trying to find him in all these clouds. Just our blasted unlucky day, Dave, I'm afraid."

"It isn't over yet!" Dawson grated, and banked the Vultee westward. "I'm going to have another look at those Albuquerque Cays. I—I refuse to give them up as a lost cause. I swear they're right in the middle of this confounded mystery."

With a savage nod for emphasis, Dawson sent the attack bomber rocketing back toward the short chain of green and brown islands sticking up out of the blue water. He was still half a mile from the most southern one when suddenly Freddy Farmer's hand came crashing down on his shoulder, and the English youth's voice cried out wildly in his ears.

"On this side of that first island, Dave! To the right! That strip of beach. There's a crashed plane there. Can you see it? Its tail is sticking up out of the sand. And, I say! There's something white on the beach. It looks like a letter—

the letter H! What in the world is that supposed to mean?"

Dave was too excited to speak for a moment. He had picked out the wreck of the plane on the beach, and the big letter "H" on the sand close to it.

"That's H for help!" he cried. "The pilot of that job must be still alive. Crashed and got marooned. And, Freddy! Unless I'm nuts, that broken off tail sticking up is the tail of a Vultee. Holy smoke! We must be blind not to have seen it before."

"Worse than that!" Freddy shouted. "But I'd almost swear it wasn't there. That's impossible, of course. But I don't see how we could have missed it. I—"

The English youth cut himself off short, and both of them stared down at the tattered figure of a man who came stumbling out of the thick underbrush waving both hands in a beseeching gesture.

"That settles it!" Dave cried. "That fellow does need help. And we're going to give it to him."

As Dave spoke the words he hauled back the Cyclone's throttle and began to lose altitude fast. He let the Vultee glide out to sea for a bit,

then banked around and headed toward the far
end of the beach, away from the crash. There
he banked once more until he was in line with
the strip of packed sand beach. Then he let his
wheels down, and glided gently forward and
down.

His landing was perfect. Not a single bounce.
He undid his safety and 'chute harness, and
legged out of the plane with Freddy. The man
in tattered clothes was stumbling toward them
head down.

"Take it easy!" Dave called out cheerfully.
"No rush, now. We're here to take you off."

"But there is a rush, my two little friends, a
most urgent reason for speed. But first you will
both put your hands in the air!"

For a second the sandy beach seemed to fall
away from beneath Dave's feet. He heard
Freddy Farmer's tight gasp, but he didn't
bother to glance at his pal. His eyes were glued
to the man in tattered clothes before him. The
man had jerked up his head at the last moment,
and a small but very deadly Luger had suddenly appeared in his right hand as though by
magic. And the muzzle of the Luger moved
back and forth from Dave's stomach to
Freddy's.

CHAPTER FIFTEEN

Nazi Cunning

IT SEEMED TO Dave that he stood there for hours
staring dumbfoundedly at the man holding the
Luger. The man was light-complexioned and
had flaxen hair. His smile was more of a leer,
but when he spoke it was perfect English that
came out from between his lips.

"So you did consent to help me *this* time!" the
man said, and broadened his smile. "That was
very nice of you. I had no idea the plane carried
you two, but I had to put up my little trap, anyway. You were much, much too interested in
that Arado. And its pilot hasn't enough gas to
keep him flying around forever. So! And of
course, I am delighted with what I've caught in
my trap. Don't move, either of you, or it will
be death now, and not later!"

Dave heard the man's words as though they
came from a thousand miles away. His head was
spinning. Guns were pounding in his brain, and
great bells were clanging furiously. For a crazy
instant he tried to tell himself that this was all
just a weird nightmare, and that he would wake

up in a nice safe bed 'most any minute. A nightmare it was, indeed. But it was reality, nevertheless—cold, stark, heart-chilling reality. On what they had believed was an errand of mercy, Freddy and he had flown right straight into the jaws of death.

Stunned beyond movement, he remained perfectly still while the man with the Luger slid around behind and removed his service automatic, and Freddy's, too. Through eyes that seemed to ache with his own misery, he glanced down the beach at what he had thought was a crashed Vultee. It wasn't a Vultee at all, only a make-believe one fashioned out of strips of wood with war painted cloth stretched over them to give the desired effect from the air. Then the man circled around back front and was facing them again. Dave stared at the almost peaches and cream skin of the face and hands, and at the flaxen hair.

"The Cub's pilot!" he heard his own voice gasp out. "You were flying that Taylor Cub and tried to get us in under those two armed Wacos!"

"Quite true," the man said, and beamed. "And congratulations on your gunnery, Captains Dawson and Farmer. Those two fools deserved what they received. They flew their aircraft like two children. But we mustn't waste time here."

The man gestured with his gun for Dave and Freddy to walk in front of him. But Dave was still gripped by his trance. He couldn't move. He could only stare at the man he had seen across the air space thousands of miles from this spot, and only a week ago. Less than a week, in fact!

"Walk!" the man with the Luger barked, though the smile remained on his lips. "Colonel Welsh sent you down here to find out things, didn't he? Well, then, let's find them out. But of course, there'll be no report made to the dear Colonel. You American Intelligence men! Such stupid fools. Every bit as stupid as the British!"

The man leered at Freddy Farmer as he spoke the last. The English youth regarded him coldly, face expressionless.

"A matter of opinion, Seven-Eleven," he said quietly. "And that's who you are, isn't it?"

The man with the Luger looked pleased. He lost his sneer for a moment while he beamed all over the place.

"I like the name the Americans give me," he said, as though he were tasting something good.

"It is very nice. But in Germany—there, and to all my agents, I am Captain Karl von Stutgardt. You have heard of *that* name, no?"

Heard of it? Dave wished he had a penny for every time he had heard the name, Captain Karl von Stutgardt, mentioned! He'd be a very rich man. Von Stutgardt was a name as famous, or as infamous, as that of Himmler. From Norway to Libya, and from Dublin to Bucharest, Karl von Stutgardt had reaped human lives as a farmer might reap wheat, by the thousands upon thousands. So this was the ruthless Nazi agent who could well be Satan's roommate? Red rage smouldered in Dawson as he eyed the man. And perhaps some of that rage showed in his face, for von Stutgardt's eyes suddenly narrowed slightly, and they took on a vicious gleam.

"If you wish, Captain Dawson," he said softly, and pointed the Luger straight at the Yank ace's heart. "Though you may not realize it, you, and your swine English friend, have given me much trouble in the past. It is my personal desire to make you suffer a little before I remove you from this war forever. However, if you wish to be foolish, then you will die quickly."

The words sounded like chunks of ice clicking against each other. Dave forced a grin to his lips and held the man with his eyes.

"Go ahead," he said evenly. "Pull the trigger. We both know, *now,* that it isn't going to be very long for you, von Stutgardt."

The Nazi started slightly, and he seemed to shoot a fearful glance out to sea. But he had control of himself almost instantly. He shrugged, grinned, and gestured again with the Luger.

"Talk is cheap," he sneered. "And you came here to see things, didn't you? Then let us not waste any more time. Walk ahead of me to that path leading away from the beach."

Von Stutgardt pointed toward a beaten path that led off through a break in the heavy undergrowth that lined the beach. As the two air aces started walking toward it they saw three figures come out of the undergrowth at the far end of the beach and trot over toward the faked airplane crash. In a matter of seconds they had it dismantled, and were carrying the parts away out of sight.

"Just a couple of babes in arms, we are, Freddy!" Dave murmured bitterly. "We took it hook, line, and sinker. I could sure kick myself plenty, right now."

"All my fault, Dave," the English youth grunted. "After all, I spotted it first, you know."

Dave started to speak, but at that exact moment he caught a flash glimpse of von Stutgardt's face out of the corner of his eye. The Nazi agent was grinning like an ape, and obviously tickled silly over the mental discomfort of his prisoners. Dave grinned also, but inwardly.

"Well, it doesn't matter much, Freddy," he said to his English pal in a low voice. "When we don't return X-62 will *know* that we were right. And he'll start the wheels turning at once, of course."

Freddy Farmer blinked and a blank expression spread over his face, but only for a brief instant. He either caught Dave's quick wink, or caught onto the play of words by himself.

"Yes, that's true," he grunted. "Too bad we can't be in on the climax of things, but that's the way with a blasted war, I fancy. However, we did manage to get our part of the job completed, so that's something, I guess."

"It's a lot," Dave said. "In my book, it's plenty. But it was nice to have known you, pal. We've had some swell times together."

"Quite!" Freddy Farmer replied. "It was all

top-hole while it lasted. And, who knows? Perhaps it isn't over yet. For us, I mean."

Dave nodded, but didn't say anything. He had sneaked another flash look at von Stutgardt out the corner of his eye. And there was no longer a pleased look on the Nazi's face. On the contrary, the man now wore a look of sullen rage tempered just a little by a glint of worry in his eyes.

Then Dave stopped sneaking quick glances at the man, for they had passed through the rim of underbrush and were approaching a series of man-made clearings in the tropical trees that covered the island. At first glance Dave could hardly believe his eyes. And when he took a second look he was sure that he must be dreaming. But it was not the results of any dream, or mirage, that he saw spread out before him. Instead, it was the most perfectly camouflaged flying field he had ever seen in his life, a flying field that had been built in sections so that enough trees would be left completely to hide everything from the air.

To be exact, the flying field really consisted of two long runways cut through the trees, and packed down firm. The runways ran from east to west across the island, and the take off end was blocked off by strips of painted camouflage cloth. The strips of cloth had only to be pulled to the side and there was an opening that looked right out onto the beach and the blue Carribbean beyond. At the other end of the two runways was a group of huts built under the trees. Staring at them, Dave saw that a couple of them, the fronts being open, were filled with H.E. bombs of five hundred to a thousand pound size. There were also aerial torpedoes, and an unlimited quantity of German made incendiary bombs.

All that, however, he simply gave but a sweeping glance. What brought him up to a dead stop, and caused him to gasp in dumbfounded amazement was the sight of ten Vultee attack bombers pulled in in line under the trees. Two of them were still without wings, but a group of bull-necked, head-shaven men were in the very act of fitting the wings in place. A couple of other bull-necked figures were busy painting U. S. Air Corps insignia on the eight other Vultees. And not only that, they were painting on the Squadron insignia of the Ninety-Sixth Attack Unit, based at Colon.

"Interesting sight, isn't it?" Dave heard von Stutgardt's jeering voice in his ears. "It has taken us a long time to collect those planes, and more trouble than I care to talk about. But we have them at last, and so that is all that matters. Yes, indeed! A most interesting sight. Most interesting."

Dave made no comment. He didn't dare let himself speak. He was pretty sure that the mystery he and Freddy had been tracking down was no longer a mystery. There it was in plain view before his eyes. In spite of his efforts to control his jangled nerves, a shiver ran through him, and von Stutgardt's mocking laugh made the blood pound in his temples.

"What a shame you cannot report all this to dear Colonel Welsh, Captain Dawson!" the German murmured with feigned sadness in his voice. "He would be *so* pleased! But as one of you just mentioned, that's the way with war. Victory goes to the strongest side. And Germany is the mightiest nation on the face of this earth. And we shall own all of this earth in a very short time."

"That's taking in a lot of territory," Dave said to him coldly. "I wouldn't bet on it, if I were you. It might backfire in your face. Or maybe you haven't caught on—yet?"

The anger and worry flashed in the German's face again. He stared hard and long at Dawson.

He seemed about to speak several times, but each time he clamped his lips shut, and said nothing.

"We will talk more of that, later," he finally did speak out. "For the present you two can rest, and spend a little time with your thoughts, which I do not believe will be very pleasant. I have other things to do. The hour of my greatest triumph is close at hand, and I—"

The Nazi let his words trail off. He just shrugged to convey their meaning, whatever that might have been. He nodded his head and motioned with his Luger for Dave and Freddy to walk over toward the nearest of the huts built in under the trees. They were some twenty-five yards from it when a figure garbed in the uniform of a Luftwaffe lieutenant pilot came running out of one of the other huts, and up to von Stutgardt.

"The contact plane radioes it must land at once, *Herr* Captain," the man spoke in German. "He asks if it is now safe to approach the secret landing basin."

"Perfectly safe, now!" von Stutgardt snapped back at him. "Tell him to come on in, and see that the men place camouflage over his seaplane the instant he has landed and has taxied up the inlet."

Both Dave and Freddy understood the words spoken in the German tongue, but they only half listened. They were staring agate-eyed at the young Luftwaffe lieutenant.

"So a lot more is clear, now!" Dave grated impulsively.

"Quite!" he heard Freddy Farmer echo. "And the blighter was right in front of our eyes!"

The young Luftwaffe pilot turned and regarded them with grinning lips and hate-filled eyes.

"Your good luck has come to an end at last, you two war-mongering dogs!" he snarled. "Now it is our turn. When we—"

"That is enough, *Herr Leutnant!*" von Stutgardt cut in harshly. "You talk too much. Go contact the U-boat's plane at once!"

The young Luftwaffe pilot gulped, flushed, then saluted stiffly and beat a hasty retreat back to the hut. Dave stared after him and felt ice cold anger in his heart. The last time he had seen that youth had been at the Air Corps Base at Albuquerque, New Mexico. The youth had not been a Nazi pilot then. He had been a U. S. Air Corps pilot—and the officer in charge of the check-in booth!

CHAPTER SIXTEEN

Wings of Doom

DAVE DAWSON'S thoughts were like so many rats gnawing away at his brain. His whole body was filled with icy shivers, and his stomach felt full of lumps of cold lead. But it was not fear that caused that conglomeration of emotion. On the contrary it was the sense of defeat, and of seemingly utter helplessness and hopelessness, that caused him to feel as he did.

He was sitting with Freddy Farmer on the rough board floor of one of the frontless huts under the trees. From there he could look out and see everything that was going on; look out and see many things that were like white hot knives turning in his heart. He watched bombs being fitted to some of the Vultees, and aerial torpedoes being fitted to the others. And watching over the efforts of the bull-necked mechanics were nine Luftwaffe pilots, and von Stutgardt.

Yes, both he and Freddy could look out and see all that was taking place, but neither of them could do anything about it, that is, unless they wanted to die instantly. Stationed some ten yards in front of the hut, and each a little to one side, were two Nazi guards. Each guard was armed with the deadly Nazi portable machine gun. And both guns were trained dead on them. So were the eyes of the two guards. They watched unwinking, like a couple of cobras waiting to strike, Dave told himself.

Sure, they could look out and see all that was taking place. They could even get up and *try* to go closer for a better look—if they wanted to! Von Stutgardt had not had them bound up. Their legs and their arms were free of ropes, or anything like that. It was strictly up to them whether they wished to live a little longer—or die at once.

"That dirty blighter who was at the Albuquerque Base!" Freddy Farmer suddenly broke a five minute silence between them. "I think I could almost die happy, if I could only give that beggar what he deserves first. We've certainly made a mess of things, Dave. But goodness knows, we had little enough to go on."

Dave nodded absently and stared out beyond the group of planes at an eleventh plane partly hidden by the tree growth beyond. It was a seaplane, a Nazi Arado. In other words, the same seaplane Freddy and he had lost in that flock of fluffy clouds high in the air. Not over half an hour ago he had heard it come down to a landing. And he had seen it taxi up a small inlet of water and come to a stop where it now rested, completely hidden from any patrolling eyes above. As he stared at it the gnawing ache in his heart increased. The Nazis were so darn cunning, so confoundedly clever and thorough. They left nothing to chance. Not they! This secret base here was a perfect example of Nazi war technique. Everything built out of sight. An expert job of camouflaging. U.S. planes could patrol the skies above, and U. S. Navy ships could control the waters all about—and nobody would even begin to suspect that the Nazis had this powerful air unit secretly based within a two hundred and fifty mile striking distance of the so very vital Panama Canal!

The Panama Canal! Dave groaned and shivered again as the name flashed through his brain. He could only guess, of course, but he was positive he could guess the right answers. Von Stutgardt's plans were as simple as they were terrifyingly disastrous in extent. One swift devastating blow that would completely fool the Canal Zone defense until it was too late—

Dave shook his head savagely and refused to

complete the horrible thought picture. He looked at Freddy and saw that the English youth was watching him closely. Freddy smiled and winked.

"Chin up, old thing," Freddy murmured. "I seem to recall we've been in one or two tight spots before. At least the blighter hasn't shot us yet. That's something. Wants to crow over us, of course. Nazi vanity when he believes he's on top. More satisfying than food and drink to those rotters. Perhaps something—"

Freddy gestured the last, and Dave returned his smile.

"Perhaps something will!" he said grimly. "It's got to. The old brain is spinning pretty much right now. But one of us has got to come up with something. And I don't think we've got much time to work the think box, either. Boy! What I wouldn't give for three minutes in that hut over there!"

Freddy looked in the direction of Dave's pointed finger, and then back at him.

"Why that hut?" he asked. "Personally, I'd choose that one still half filled with bombs. I could make a beautiful noise, and have things knocked about no end, if I could be left alone in that hut for a bit."

"I'll still take my hut," Dave grunted. "It happens to be their radio shack. Give me three minutes and I'd have a couple of hundred bombers and ground fighters on their way out here. Just three minutes at the mike, or the key. Maybe two would be all I'd need."

"In that case," Freddy murmured, and stared across at the hut indicated, "we'll have to see if we can't arrange something along that line."

"Yes, sure," Dave sighed. "We might ask von Stutgardt, even. Here he comes over to start that crowing you were talking about. Boy! Wouldn't I love to push him right in that ugly face of his. The majority of Nazis certainly were behind the door when the good looks were passed out, weren't they?"

"Down in the cellar, no doubt," Freddy grunted, "plotting fresh carnage and chaos. Well, here he comes, anyway."

Von Stutgardt strode up to their hut with a smirking smile on his face that stretched from ear to ear. He came to a halt a little distance away so that he was not in line with either of the guards' guns, and stood there staring at them for a moment.

"You are perfectly comfortable?" he suddenly spoke in his mocking voice. "Sorry I can't let you move about at will. But that might prove a little dangerous. Of course, now that you have had the chance to observe things, you realize what is about to take place, eh?"

"Sure!" Dave shot at him. "We've guessed what you *think* is about to take place. But that's a different kind of cheese, von Stutgardt. Plenty different!"

The German looked at him, and laughed.

"Stop trying to bolster up your courage, Captain Dawson," he jeered. "There is nothing that can stop us, keep us from our great triumph, now. Yes, I will admit that a few days ago, when you two were receiving your orders from Colonel Welsh, I was a little worried about just how much you knew. And the other day when another one of your stupid agents came poking his nose about here, I wondered if my well laid plans were really in danger. I tricked him down, the same way I tricked you. He was a fool, and put up a fight. Naturally, I was forced to kill him, and have him buried."

"Poor Marble," Freddy Farmer murmured. "Then he *did* know something."

"Yes, that was his name," von Stutgardt grunted. "We knew he was working with an agent named Tracey, in the Canal Zone. I had

Marble watched, while I trailed Tracey north-ward. Tell me something! Why did he make that trip north so suddenly? I have wondered a lot about that since—since I ordered his finish."

The question was directed at Dawson, but the Yank ace didn't reply at once. He wondered, too. But what did it matter now? Tracey was dead, and his real reason for making that sud-den trip northward to contact Colonel Welsh would remain another of the war's unrevealed secrets. Perhaps it was to arrange for a small force attack on this secret Nazi base, or, perhaps for some other reason. Who could tell? And what did it matter? Tracey was dead—and von Stutgardt was about to strike his Panama Canal paralyzing blow. But Dave didn't let any of that show in his face as he returned the Nazi's look.

"Wouldn't you like to know?" he grunted. "Well, don't worry! You'll find out soon enough!"

"Quite!" Freddy Farmer exclaimed quickly, picking up Dawson's lead. "And no doubt you'll find out sooner than you think."

But it all seemed to have no visible effect on Captain Karl von Stutgardt. He continued to sneer, and there was haughty disdain in his glittering eyes.

"Very amusing," he said. "But I, too, am very well acquainted with the art of bluffing. You little fools! Have I not had you watched every minute of the time? Have I not been able practically to read your thoughts? Bah! If it had not been necessary to get rid of you so that the U-boat contact plane could land and give me my final orders from Berlin, I would have let you fly back to your Colon Base—and die with the others there. But I had to let that contact plane land. And also—I could not find it in my heart to let you two die without having found out *anything*. That is one of my weak points. The Fuehrer has often told me that I am too generous to my enemies. But it will all be over soon, so I can afford to be a little generous. Of course, not *too* generous, you understand?"

The German thought that was a great joke, and threw back his head and laughed loudly. Dave measured the distance between them with his eyes, but savagely fought down the almost berserk urge for action. This wasn't the time for action. At this moment von Stutgardt held all the cards, and he was playing them close to his chest. Later, please God! But not right at this moment.

"Okay, have it your way, von Stutgardt," he said, and shrugged. "You're a pilot, I suppose? You're going to lead this sneak bomb and aerial torpedo raid, in American planes, on the Canal?"

"Of course I am!" the German cried wildly. "And how your swine American comrades there will be surprised! They will see us come over, believe us to be from their Ninety-Sixth Attack Squadron, and before they realize what has happened—!"

The German paused and gestured a series of mighty explosions with his two hands.

"So!" he shouted. "There will be no more Panama Canal. We will return here as soon as possible, and there will be U-boats waiting to take us away to other fields of battle. But I have neglected to mention the part you two will play."

The Nazi paused again and leered at them, his two eyes like burning coals of hatred.

"I will arrange for you two to be able to make a complete report to the dear Colonel Welsh, when you three meet again *after death!*" the man suddenly cried. "You will be able to tell him everything, *then.* All the details on how the Canal was destroyed. An eye witness account it shall be, because you two are going to see it all with your eyes. Yes, as my personal guests."

Von Stutgardt had another laughing spell, and it was a couple of moments before he continued.

"That is very good, my personal guests!" he chuckled. "In a Vultee there is room for three— a pilot, a radio man, and the rear gunner. So I shall take you two along with me. And when it is all over, when you have seen all there is to see, I will dump you out over Ninety-Six's field. Or course you will not be wearing parachutes, and you will be bound hand and foot. But you will reach the ground, of course, and there should be enough of you left to be identified. You know, I wonder if dear Colonel Welsh will weep very much when he finds out. You have failed him miserably this time, you know."

"This time isn't over yet, you dirty rotter!" Freddy Farmer blurted out. "But continue with your little speech. We are amused, too. Very much *indeed*. Go ahead, you blasted murderer! Have your sport *while you may!*"

Von Stutgardt's eyes seemed to shoot off sparks as he glared at Freddy. For a moment Dave feared the Nazi was going to use his Luger, and he got set to hurl himself at the man.

Von Stutgardt's face was white with rage, and his upper lip was trembling. But he did not use the Luger he clutched in his right hand. With a tremendous effort he gained mastery over his emotions. He slowly lowered the Luger and twitched one corner of his mouth in what was supposed to be a mocking smile.

"I will dump you out last, my swine English friend!" he bit off at Freddy. "That will add to my pleasure, to watch you die last. But I waste too much time here. Ask the guards for anything you like. You won't get it, of course. Sweet dreams, then, you two stupid little fools—until tomorrow at dawn!"

With a curt nod for each of them, and a parting smirk, von Stutgardt swung around on his heel and walked rapidly away.

"So it's tomorrow at dawn, eh?" Freddy Farmer murmured, and stared squint-eyed off into space. "Nasty beggar, what?"

"A low-down bum of the first water," Dave grunted. "But I've got the feeling that he's not as happy as he'd like to be. That bird is worried, Freddy. He tried to cover up with his tough words, but he's worried. We got under his skin, and he doesn't feel so good."

"No doubt," Freddy said with a sigh and a

wry smile. "But I could name two others who don't feel so good about things, either."

"Don't bother!" Dawson groaned. "I can get it on the first guess!"

CHAPTER SEVENTEEN

Eagle Lightning

THE TROPICAL SUN was still a way above the western lip of the world, but because of the canopy of dense trees and other growth that covered the island the light on the ground was pale and silverish, and long slender shadows crisscrossed each other. Slumped down on the rough wood floor beside Freddy Farmer, Dave closed his eyes tight for the umpty-umpth time, and searched his tortured brain for a possible way out of this tightest of all traps that had ever caught him between its jaws.

But once again his aching brain was unable to conjure up anything that wouldn't result in practically instant death. It was just no use, it seemed, even to try to think, for the stone wall was ever there in his brain. On the other hand, though, it was impossible not to think, and so the countless soul-stabbing thoughts went around and around in a vicious circle.

Hardly realizing that he was doing so, he went back in memory and retraced every step of this mad, fruitless journey that had begun in

Colonel Welsh's office in San Francisco. What had happened to the agent who was supposed to follow Freddy and him to Albuquerque? Had he perhaps had engine trouble, and been unable to get off in time? And had it been accidental trouble? But why wonder about that small item? What good would it do him now to know? None at all. But he hoped Colonel Welsh's agent came out of it all right.

And that fake message the Colonel had sent to Washington as a means of baiting the trap for whoever had tapped the phone lines. Had it worried those listening in? He thought it had. And he was certain that Captain Karl von Stutgardt was still worried. That was one thing Colonel Welsh had figured wrong, however. Seven-Eleven *had* been in the States all that time. And how bitter to realize now that he had been the pilot of that Taylor Cub! If Freddy and he had only known! What a terrible menace to the civilized world they could have removed right then and there. But why think of that now, either?

And that supposedly Second Lieutenant Miller who had served as check-in officer at Albuquerque! He had fired at Freddy from that rifle range. Had had that Sergeant take over his post and slipped over there. And it had been Miller, of course, who had hidden that pencil incendiary bomb aboard the Flying Fortress. Easy for him to have done that, for he had the run of the Base. Nobody would have wondered about the movements of a check-in officer. Second Lieutenant Miller? More likely it was *Oberleutnant Meuller,* of the Nazi Luftwaffe!

And now this place! A secret base of the most hated nation in the history of the world. A secret base within easy striking distance of the Panama Canal. How simple it all would be for von Stutgardt and his nine other vultures. Their planes would of course be taken for Ninety-Six aircraft returning from patrol. Then before anybody realized the truth of things, these devil men would strike. Their bombs and their aerial torpedoes would go hurtling down, and in one blinding flash every lock from Colon to Balboa would be destroyed, and the Canal put out of use for months and months to come—and maybe for all time!

Dave groaned in spite of himself and hitched up on one elbow. He stared at the two armed guards, and they stared back unwinkingly at him. Just looking at them made him see red, and caused a wild, completely insane recklessness to steal through his body. He forced himself to look the other way. He twisted around a bit and absently stared at the back of the hut. There were two windows, but only the frames. Neither glass nor netting had been put in as yet. Beyond the windows he could see the tangle of untouched tropical growth. It was bathed in weird light and grotesque shadows. He stared at it, and the reckless spirit within him grew stronger and started his heart to thumping against his ribs.

He glanced at Freddy, but the English youth sat with his arms folded on his knees, and his bent head resting on his folded arms. He might be asleep, but Dave knew that wasn't so. Freddy was simply sitting there suffering the tortures of the doomed, too. Dave took a deep breath and then slowly got up onto his feet.

"Got to stretch my legs," he said. "They feel ready to snap off any second."

He spoke the words with a smile, but he was watching the two guards closely out of the corner of one eye. They stiffened to the alert as he stood up, and he could almost see their hands tighten on their sub-machine guns. But he paid them no visible attention, however. He stretched both hands above his head, and yawned loudly.

His heart was well up in his throat by now. Were the guards going to do something, or weren't they? He looked down at Freddy again, shrugged for the benefit of the ever watching guards, and then jammed his hands in his pockets and started to saunter about the limited amount of floor space. He walked with his head bent and his eyes fixed on the floor boards, as though he were fed up with everything, and just didn't care a hoot what happened next.

As a matter of fact, though, he kept darting glances in all directions, particularly out the two rear windows. He saw then for sure that there was nothing but heavy jungle growth to the rear of the hut. And because of the heavy growth the shadows out there were deepening more and more by the minute. His heartbeat was hitting full speed when presently he sauntered back to Freddy and slumped down on the floor.

"You're a lazy bum, pal!" he said with a laugh. "Why don't you stretch your legs? Just sitting there moping won't change a thing. The party's all over as far as we're concerned."

Freddy lifted his head and shot him a hard glance. Dave slowly winked the eye that the watching guards couldn't see. Then, leaning forward, he balanced both elbows on his knees and put his two hands up to his face with the fingers spread apart. He could look out between the spread fingers, but his two palms completely concealed his mouth. He stared vacantly off into space for a long time, until he saw the guards relax a bit, though they did not remove their steadfast, unwinking gaze.

"There's just one play we can make, Freddy," he then whispered into his two palms held in front of his mouth. "Just one play. It may fall flat and get us nailed deader than frozen fish. But, Freddy, we've just got to do *something!* We just can't sit here and let von Stutgardt dish it out at dawn! Right?"

He heard Freddy groan and roll over on his stomach. The English youth's movement brought his head close to Dave's knees. Freddy rested his forehead on his two palms so that he was looking down between his forearms at the floor boards.

"Right!" Dave presently heard the faint whisper. "I'm willing to try anything, and blast the cost to us. I'll even charge those two blighters out there, if you think that's best. But have you any idea, Dave? Anything that offers a little bit of a chance?"

"Just an idea, that's about all," Dave breathed into his palms. "And we've got to play it soon, while they're still keeping us here. When it gets dark they'll probably truss us up for the business at dawn. Freddy! The two rear windows. We've got to dive through them before those guards can pull their triggers. We can try it, this way."

Dave paused and took away one of his hands to scratch the top of his head. He yawned and stretched both arms, and then braced his spread fingers against the upper part of his face again. The guards still watched him, but there was no suspicion or uneasiness in their pig-like eyes.

"This way, Freddy," he whispered again. "We get up to stretch our legs. I tried it, and the guards didn't seem to mind. We act tired and fed up, and not caring what happens next. We slouch around for a good ten minutes, enough time to get the guards used to us moving around. Then when you're in front of one window, and I'm in front of the other, I'll sneeze. That'll be the go signal. Freddy. When I sneeze, we both dive head first through a window in nothing flat. Got that?"

"Got it." The two words just barely reached Dave's ears. "And then what?"

"Then it's up to you, pal," Dave breathed.

"That radio hut, I mean. Our first hope is to radio to Colon and get bombers out here on the jump. You know the usual SOS signal. Get word to Colon Base. And maybe some Navy ships close by will pick it up, too. Now, I'll cover for you so that you can sneak around back and get into that radio hut. As soon as we land outside the window I'll turn sharp left and make a lot of noise getting away. You hug the ground until they're in full flight after me. And then— then do your stuff, Freddy. And good luck to you. Okay?"

"Definitely not!" came the instant reply. "I'll do the covering up—if we escape the guards' bullets. The radio idea was yours in the first place. Besides, I can't operate those gadgets the way you can. No, Dave! You work the SOS business. I'll draw the blighters away from you. No arguments, please. I honestly can do that best, Dave. I'd stand a much better chance of throwing them off and circling back to joining you than you would. You know that's true, too."

Dave didn't reply for a moment. He realized full well that Freddy Farmer did speak the truth. He knew it from experience in the past. English though he was, Freddy Farmer was almost the equal of an American Indian scout when it came to moving about in woods and heavy undergrowth. His movements were those of a shadow, and twice as silent. Yes, Freddy could do better drawing off the pursuers. And, too, he wasn't so hot at the radio business, particularly a key wireless. But drawing off the pursuers was the most dangerous job. He stood about one chance in a hundred of not being spotted and brought to earth by gun fire. Still—

"It must be that way, Dave!" came the whisper. "I insist! We've got to do it my way. Blast it, Dave! It's the only way possible. This is no time to think of each other. Don't you see?"

Dave bit his lips, but the absolute truth of Freddy's words was too much for him. After all, what mattered most was the fate of the Panama Canal.

"Okay," he finally said. "But if anything happens to you, pal, I'll—"

He couldn't finish. Then he felt Freddy's head pressing lightly against his left knee, and he knew that Freddy understood without being told. Dave swallowed hard and wondered if the guards could see tears showing in his eyes. For a crazy moment he was tempted to call it all off. Perhaps there was some other way out. Perhaps at dawn he could add to von Stutgardt's obvious worries, and get the Nazi to postpone striking his terrible blow. Maybe that crack about X-62 could be used again. Of course, Dave didn't know of anybody who was known as X-62. But mentioning that, as von Stutgardt herded them up from the beach, had made worried lights flash in the Nazi's eyes. The Nazi didn't know the truth about X-62, and maybe—just maybe—

Dave let the rest slide as Freddy Farmer groaned again and rolled over on his back, and then up to a sitting position.

"Did stretching your legs help any?" the English youth asked in a loud voice. "Very well, I'll try it. But, frankly, I think it's silly to worry about our health now. It's all over for us. We two are finished, blast it!"

Freddy spoke the last in distinct German, and openly glared at the two guards. If they didn't understand the English words they most certainly understood the German words, and Freddy's glare. They both grinned wolfishly and nodded their heads slightly. Freddy glared at them for a bit longer, then coldly turned his back on them and started slouching about the hut floor. Dave glanced at the guards, saw them chuckling in amusement at Freddy's obvious discomfort of body and mind, and hoped he could put on as good an act as his pal.

He remained where he was for a couple of minutes, a perfect picture of dejected defeat and misery. Then he sighed and got slowly up on his own feet. But he didn't start walking immediately. He just stood there a moment absently rubbing his two hands up and down the sides of his face, and staring sad-eyed out past the guards. When he could tell that they were no more on the alert than usual, he stopped rubbing his face, jammed his hands in his pockets, grunted, and started shuffling about the place in a circle.

One minute—two minutes—three minutes ticked slowly by, and it was all that Dave could do to stop from screaming at the top of his voice. Every nerve and muscle in him was drawn tight, close to the snapping point. Each second had seemed an hour longer, and each minute a whole eternity. With every step he took he was seized with the wild desire to sneeze the signal and dive headlong through one of the windows. Anything, *anything* to break this torturing suspense. Anything so long as it meant action. That was all he craved, now, and nuts to the results.

He maintained a steely grip on himself, however. Three minutes weren't half enough to soothe away any sneaking suspicions that the two guards might have. Every time he snapped a glance their way from up under his brows he saw that they were tensed and watching Freddy and him as two cats might watch a couple of mice. Not time, yet, for the do or die effort. Not until the guards got used to their shuffling around and relaxed a little. They were still on the alert too much. Their trigger fingers were still too itchy and ready.

Four minutes—five—six—seven! When had he started this slouching around to get exercise? Had it been yesterday, or last week, or last year? He didn't dare look at Freddy for fear the guards would see his look and take it for some kind of a signal. It was only seven minutes. *Only* seven? That was all the minutes there were in the world, wasn't it?

Eight minutes—nine! Praise be to Allah! The guards were relaxing a little. One of them had shifted his feet to a more comfortable stance. And his sub-machine gun was pointing a little more toward the ground. The other guard, too, was seemingly getting just a little bored with the prisoner parade. He let go of his gun with one hand to slap at a fly buzzing around his face. It was making him wink for the first time.

Ten minutes—eleven! Dave saw Freddy close to one of the windows—real close. He took a quick side step that took him to within two feet of his window. He shot a quick glance at the two guards—and sneezed!

In the next couple of seconds a hundred different things seemed to happen at the same time. His whole body seemed to explode like many firecrackers as his coiled spring muscles let go, and his feet left the floor and he dived headlong through the window. He misjudged the opening by a hair and felt sharp pain as his shoulder cracked against the jamb. He caught a flash glimpse of Freddy going out the other window like a flying fish above the crest of a wave. Then there was a roaring blast of noise in back of him. It was as though the three-sided hut were crashing down about his ears. And his head was suddenly filled with the whistle and zinging of many unseen bullets. Slivers of wood flew past him, and then—and then he was landing like a cat on all fours on the ground below the window, and heavy tropical growth was clutching out at him.

For a brief instant there was no air in his

lungs, and there were dancing lights before his eyes. Then somebody grabbed his arm. It was Freddy Farmer, and the English youth's voice was in his ears.

"Good luck, old man! I'll take care of the blighters!"

And in the next flash second Freddy Farmer was gone. He wasn't there any more. There was just heavy tangy-smelling tropical island undergrowth. And from a good distance away came the calling voice.

"Over here, Dave! Run! There's a path. . . !"

The last was drowned out by the thunderous roar of gunfire—gunfire that seemed to come right out of the top of Dave's head!

Chapter Eighteen

Thundering Revenge

"Over there! Hurry! The swine will get to the beach! Fire your machine gun, Fritz! Perhaps our bullets will reach them through these cursed trees. *Goot!* They are like two shafts of lightning, only faster!"

The words were screamed in German, and seemed inches from Dave's ringing ears. They, of course, came from the mouth of one of the guards who stood not three feet from Dave's body hugging the ground underneath heavy undergrowth. He could even see the booted foot of one guard, and his heart seemed to jam up his throat as he waited in fear that the guard would turn and step right on him. Hugging the ground though he was, and completely covered by undergrowth, he felt as though he were standing right in the middle of a glass house. And with every ticking second he expected to hear one of the machine guns snarl, and feel the white hot bullets biting into his body.

Then suddenly the guards started plunging off through the thick tropical growth. They called out to one another in the bad light, and a few seconds later there were other voices. Other Nazis had taken up the chase.

"Dear God! Don't let them get Freddy. Protect him, dear God! Please!"

Dave didn't speak the words. His heart spoke them as he slid up onto his hands and knees. He crouched there for an instant and listened to the sounds that now seemed far away because of the thickness of the island growth that blanketed all sound. Then he got up to his feet, sucked air into his aching lungs, and shot off in the opposite direction, body bent and head held well down. He traveled through the growth in a straight line for perhaps fifty yards. Then when he saw that he was well beyond the rim of the group of huts at the head of the double runway, he veered off to the right, and stole close to the nearest hut. It was one that served as living quarters, but there was no one there. He turned slightly and started forward again, but dived forward instead!

One of the bull-necked mechanics had come running around the far corner of the hut. He saw Dave, but a split second too late. Dave had taken Commando training in England, and he thanked God for that training in this moment.

The top of his head hit the Nazi's chin a terrific crack. At practically the same instant Dave's iron hard fists slammed deep into the Nazi's stomach. No man could take that kind of punishment, and the bull-necked mechanic was no exception to the rule. He grunted just once and went toppling over backward. If he needed a further knockout blow he got it when Dawson's body came crashing down on top of him.

As Dave scrambed up onto his feet he took a quick look down at the prostrate mechanic and grinned, tight-lipped. The slob of a Nazi would be hearing the birdies for several hours to come. Dave started forward again, but checked himself long enough to snap a hand down and jerk free the Luger the German carried stuck in his belt.

"Seeing as how you'll not be using it for a while!" he murmured, and went darting forward again.

In just two minutes by anybody's clock he was hidden in the undergrowth that backed the radio hut. He strained his ears for sounds from within, but if there were any he couldn't hear them because of the distant roar of sound that came from German throats hot in pursuit of the still (thank God!) elusive Freddy Farmer.

"Keep him safe, dear God!" Dave whispered softly, and crawled around the rear corner of the hut on his hands and knees. "Keep him safe!"

Another few seconds and he was at the front door. He hesitated a fraction of an instant and shot a sharp look around. He thought he saw a moving figure over on the other side of the runways, but he couldn't tell for sure because of the bad light. Above the treetops there was still blue sky and sunshine, but down under the trees the light was fading fast.

Anyway, there was no time to bother about moving shadows, and so, clutching the Luger butt tighter, Dave took one quick step forward, then whirled and went inside the hut in a single leap. A figure bent over the radio started up and spun around as Dave entered. It was the former check-in officer at Albuquerque Base. Stark fear registered on the youth's face for an instant. Then it became flooded with blazing anger and hatred.

"Swine dog! I'll—"

"Shut up, and hold everything, rat!" Dave grated.

But the young Luftwaffe pilot was too engulfed in his own rage. He swung around, yanked open a table drawer and started to snatch out a gun that was inside. Maybe his fingers touched it, but maybe they didn't. Dawson didn't wait to see. He leaped forward and swung his own gun. There was the *crunch* that metal makes when it strikes jaw bone. And the Luftwaffe pilot simply folded up like a weary army cot and sank silently down onto the floor.

There was no need for a second blow, and Dave didn't waste a single split second delivering one for good measure. He simply shoved the limp figure aside with his foot and dropped into the chair. There were both mike and wireless key in front of him. The switch for the key set was thrown shut. He opened it, however, and closed the radio switch because he could talk faster than he could send by key. A second later the room was filled with the hum of the generators. Another few seconds and the tubes were warm enough for transmitting. Dave hooked the earphones over his head, and put his lips to the mike.

"SOS Colon Base!" he barked. "Emergency, Colon! Dispatch attack force at once to southern Albuquerque Cays. Nazi secret plane base here. Preparing to strike at Canal at—"

Crack!

The sound of the gun's bark, and the shower of hissing blue sparks in Dave Dawson's face, seemed to come almost simultaneously. For an instant he was completely blinded by the radio panel that had virtually exploded in his face. He kicked his chair and blindly reached for the Luger he had placed on the panel table close to his hand. But in that instant there was a second shot, and the Luger he saw through smarting eyes seemed to take off like an airplane and go falling down onto the floor.

"The third shot will be for you, of course!"

Shock fled, and common sense returned to Dave. The radio episode was finished—that is, as far as the set itself was concerned. The first bullet had smashed the main tube, and the whole panel was now giving off dirty blue smoke. He turned slowly and stared into the brittle, deadly eyes of Captain Karl von Stutgardt, who stood framed in the hut doorway. The Nazi's lips were pulled back over his teeth in a vicious snarl, but his shoulders were shaking a little. It was as though he were silently chuckling to himself. He was, for it suddenly rose to a harsh laugh.

"Too bad, Captain Dawson!" he cried. "That was a noble effort. But I couldn't allow you to

complete your little broadcast, you know. That's
a very low powered transmitter, and your voice
couldn't possibly have been heard in Colon. You
should have used the key wireless. But of course
it's too late for that now. In fact, it is too. late
for everything, as far as you're concerned, Captain Dawson!"

Dave only half listened to the words. He
knew that he was not going to die this very instant. Maybe in a minute or two, but not right
now. Von Stutgardt's vanity had to be satisfied
first. The rat from Berlin had to enjoy his crowing before he continued with his job of murder.
And murder it would be. Dave knew that he
stood as near death as he ever would. The Nazi's
Luger was pointed straight at his heart, and the
man had just proved that he was an expert shot.

But what about Freddy Farmer? That was
the thought that raced and circled about in
Dave's brain as he stood there tensed in front
of von Stutgardt's Luger. Had they caught
Freddy finally? Had they chased him clear
across the island to the beach on the other side
and then shot him down as one would shoot
down a mad dog? He couldn't hear any sounds
of voices calling out, nor the sound of gun fire
either. Freddy! Freddy, old man! I've failed

you. Failed you completely. Have you paid for it with your life? Have I brought certain death —to us both? Oh, dear God!

Dawson's agonizing thoughts were as spoken words in his brain. They came from all sides to haunt and to taunt him. He felt the blood seem to drain out of his body, leaving only the seething flames of berserk anger within him. Unconsciously he let his eyes meet von Stutgardt's again, and he saw that the Nazi was chuckling.

"Your swine English friend?" the Nazi echoed, as though he had read Dave's thoughts. "You can forget about him. I can promise you that he is dead, or soon will be. This is not a large island, you know. As a matter of fact, that is why I gave you as much freedom as I did, why I didn't tie you hand and foot. Knowing your record of stupid deeds in the past, I thought you might try some foolish move like this. So I simply waited. Why? To give us a little sport, of course. A little sport before our great day tomorrow. It is good for one's nerves when they are too tight, you know, a nice little man hunt. We Germans enjoy man hunts, you know."

"Sure!" Dave flung at him. "If the man you're hunting is unarmed. Well, I'm unarmed, von

Stutgardt. Why don't you shoot? Go ahead and get your big thrill. There'll *still* be X-62 left, you know."

Dave spoke the last on the spur of the moment, just to see how von Stutgardt's expression would change. He was disappointed. The German just stood there with his sneering smile on his face. Dave looked past him and out at the first of the Vultees at the head of the double runway.

"So you had trouble getting those planes, von Stutgardt?" he said just to keep the German talking. "I don't think it was much trouble. I saw how you got ours. You got the others the same way, didn't you?"

"That's right," the German said, and beamed. "The trouble was to get pilots from the Colon Base on solo patrol to come this far north. But we managed it, after a fashion."

"And their pilots?" Dave asked, and stared the Nazi straight in the eye.

"We wanted the planes, not the pilots!" von Stutgardt snarled back. "You think we play at war like children? Like you Americans, and the swine British? The life of an enemy to us? Nothing! I spared your life, and that dog Britisher's, simply because I wished to amuse

myself, and to let you see how stupid you were
in your efforts to trap me, the greatest secret
agent of them all. But—"

The German paused and made a little gesture
with the hand that did not hold the Luger.

"But now that I have had my little sport, and
one of you is already dead, or is dying at this
very moment, I tire of it all," the German said
presently. "You are mere children, and we Germans have a man's work to do. So—so give my
best wishes to your dear Colonel Welsh when
you meet him, Captain Dawson. And you will
be meeting him soon—for that dog is the next
on my list."

Dave saw the Luger in von Stutgardt's hand
come up an inch. He saw the Nazi's grip on the
butt tighten. He thought he saw the knuckle of
the trigger finger go white as the man started
to shoot. But he didn't hear the shot, though
there was a shot. He didn't hear it because it
came from outside the hut, and there was a ringing in his ears that drowned out all distant
sounds. He simply saw von Stutgardt twist
around as though spun by giant invisible hands.
He saw the man's Luger drop from his limp
fingers. And he saw the spurt of blood on von
Stutgardt's neck as the Nazi agent fell in

through the doorway and down onto the floor.

And in the next split second he saw a figure garbed in the work uniform of a German mechanic come leaping in over the fallen von Stutgardt.

"Phew, Dave! I was afraid that he had already shot you! You sure you're all right?"

It was three long seconds before Dave could snap himself out of his stunned trance, and pry words out of his mouth.

"Freddy!" he gasped. "Freddy Farmer? You got away from them?"

"Of course not!" Freddy panted. "This is my twin brother! Certainly I got away. Those beggars couldn't find anything unless it was stuck on the end of their big noses. I got up close to one stupid ox, and bashed him silent, and took his uniform and gun. After that it was as easy as pie. I was trying to sneak up on this blighter when I saw him raise his gun. So I had to shoot. I hope he bleeds to death. I—Good grief! The radio! Dave, did you—?"

"I didn't!" Dave groaned. "Not powerful enough. I was halfway through when he came in and shot the thing into flames right in front of my face. But let's cut this gab. I'll bless you and give you a big kiss later, pal, for saving my hide. Right now we've got a job to do all alone."

"What I've been trying to explain!" Freddy snapped, and spun around. "They're all down at the other end hunting for me in the grass. That first Vultee, eh, Dave? What say?"

"Stop asking questions!" Dave barked. "Just pick up your feet, and get going with me. Gee, Freddy! What a sweetheart and a honey you always are in the clutches!"

The English youth didn't make any comment to that. He was too busy picking up his feet, as Dave had suggested, and laying them down again. Shoulder to shoulder the two air aces raced out the door and across the clearing to the first of the bomb-loaded Vultees. Without wasting words talking it over, Dave leaped into the forward pit, and Freddy leaped into the rear pit and unhooked the swivel guns. As soon as his pants hit the seat Dave rapped open the throttle, and punched the starter button with his other hand. For a couple of seconds the starter made a grinding sound and the steel-bladed propeller rotated in a series of slow jerks. Then it caught in a rush of power and the dimly lighted clearing seemed to tremble and shake in the thunderous roar of the Wright Cyclone in the nose.

"Hang on, and be ready with those guns, Freddy!" Dave bellowed at the top of his voice, and rammed the throttle wide open.

As though the word guns had been some sort of a signal for which the unseen gods of war were waiting, the savage yammer of gunfire suddenly broke out to the left rear of the Vultee now lunging forward. Dave jerked his head around in time to see von Stutgardt coming reeling out through the radio hut door clutching a machine gun in his hands. He blazed away at the Vultee, and countless hornets of death whined by Dave's head. Then von Stutgardt stumbled and fell, and his gun stopped spitting out flame and sound.

Dave didn't wait to watch the German go sprawling. He had snapped his head front, and was biting down hard on his lower lip. The Vultee was a comet roaring along the runway now. But more guns were shooting at it from the heavy undergrowth on either side. And directly ahead was the camouflage screening for the opening out onto the beach. Dave had forgotten all about that until this moment. How strong was the screen? Would it crack them up? Would it catch on the prop blades, and bind about them, and slow up the Vultee's speed so that the plane wouldn't take off until it was down the beach and in the water? Would it—?

But there wasn't any time to answer any of those questions, much less do anything about them. Like a streak of greased lightning the whirling prop of the Vultee slashed into the netting. Things flew off in all directions for a brief instant, and then there was clear air and sunshine ahead, and Dave was hauling the plane up over the blue surface of the Caribbean.

"Like razor blades through a hair net!" Dave shouted joyfully as the aircraft mounted higher. "Always did say these Vultees were the toughest thing with wings. I—"

"Never mind the talk!" came Freddy Farmer's scream in his ears. "We got a bomb or two to drop. And there's a couple of the blighters coming up after us. It's our turn, now, Dave! And for the love of Saint George, let's get going!"

"And how!" Dave shouted, and hauled the Vultee off its climb and over and around in a dive. "And how! You keep those Nazi mosquitoes off our necks, Freddy, and I'll dump the eggs where they'll do the most good. A secret base, huh? Well, not for long. *Not for long!*"

As Dave roared out the last he pointed the

Vultee's nose straight for the spot of lush green on the island that hid the far end of the runways, and the little cluster of huts. Two Vultees came ripping out of the opening as he went rocketing down, but he didn't waste any time dropping his nose more and bringing them into his forward gun sights. Freddy would take care of those Vultees. He had a job of his own to do!

So, holding the attack bomber steady, he took it earthward at terrific speed, leveled off in the last split second allowed, and went streaking forward just off the tops of the trees. At the right instant he yanked back the bomb release lever and sent the one thousand pounds of death and doom hurtling downward. No sooner did he release the bomb than he banked sharply to the right and hauled the Vultee's nose up toward heaven.

For some strange reason everything seemed to become deathly still for a moment. It was the pressure in his ears, of course, from the violent bank and steep climb. But in a crazy sort of way it struck him as though heaven and earth had suddenly stood still, and were waiting for that bomb to hit.

Well, heaven and earth, and Dave Dawson, didn't have to wait long. Suddenly invisible giants' hands seemed to grab hold of the belly of the Vultee and fling it far out across the sky. Then came the roar of sound. It was as though the very earth had split apart in two sections and belched up all the fire and seething lava in their depths. For a moment red and white balls of light spun around before Dave's eyes, and when he could see, it was a tremendous effort to turn his head and look back down.

When he did, though, his breath caught in his throat, and cold shivers of horror shook his body from head to foot. There was no more lush green and brown on the Albuquerque Cay. There was nothing but a small ocean of seething flame and mountain clouds of yellow white smoke, edged all around by the blue of the Caribbean. A bull's-eye shot with a bomb, if there ever had been one! Dave didn't even need one guess to know that his one thousand pounder had unquestionably smacked right down on that hut that housed all the other high explosives. No, not just a thousand pound bomb exploding, but *tons* of high explosives, and not a few aerial torpedoes for good measure. That horrible flaming chaos down there was just a picture of what the Nazis had been holding in store for the Panama Canal.

"There won't be a blade of grass, even, left alive down there!" Dave heard his own lips mutter in awe. "And as for von Stutgardt, and his vulture brood, they'll never murder another—"

He didn't finish the rest. At that moment the yammer of aerial machine guns cut through his whirling thoughts. He jerked around in the seat and saw the two escaped Vultees curving up toward him with all guns blazing. He also saw Freddy Farmer snap out of his obvious trance and stop gaping down at the horrible sight below.

"Get to work and earn your pay!" Dave roared, and threw the Vultee into a snap roll. "I've done my part. Now you do yours, kid!"

The English youth didn't reply, that is, not with his lips. Instead, he spoke with his two swivel mounted machine guns. Though almost upside down, and practically standing on his ear as Dave whipped the Vultee over and down, Freddy drilled one of the Nazi flown planes dead center. It seemed to fly straight into an invisible rubber wall in the sky. It hit it and actually bounced back. Then as flames belched out and engulfed it, the plane went tumbling down into the Caribbean.

"Nice shooting!" Dave shouted, and cut the Vultee around in the opposite direction.

The remaining Nazi pilot saw him coming and tried to get out of the way. When he saw that he was trapped, he simply fired his guns blindly and then went down into a steep dive. Dave dropped down after him, but there was no need for either Freddy or him to shoot. The fear of the devil must have been in that diving Nazi's heart, because he never pulled out of his dive. He hit the surface of the Caribbean like three ton of flying brick. There was a great splash of water, but when the foam of the froth had disappeared there wasn't a sign of the plane. It, too, had disappeared, straight down.

Hauling out of his dive, Dave took one last look back at the still seething sea of flame and smoke that had been lush green, and brown, and silvery strips of beach, just a short time ago. Then with a slight shudder he turned front and put the Vultee on a crow flight course for the Air Corps Base at Colon. Then he twisted in the seat and grinned back at Freddy Farmer.

"Well, Lady Luck is still our sweetheart, Freddy!" he called out. "Your courage, and my dumb luck made it turn out swell."

"It was luck all the way!" the English youth

called back. "We came much, much too close to missing this time. Fact is, I'm wondering just how we'll be able to explain things to Colonel Welsh, and make it appear we did use our heads a little."

"Who cares?" Dave laughed. "We'll just say we did it with mirrors, or—"

Dave paused as he became conscious of a bruise ache on his right chest. He glanced down and then went pop-eyed when he saw that the right top pocket of his tunic had been ripped open. He stuck his finger in through the tear and felt a piece of metal. He pulled it out and gulped. It was the silver-filled copper disc. But it wasn't flat and smooth now. And there was more than just a pen knife scratch in the copper. The disc was bent double, and there was a big gash where the bullet had struck and ricocheted away. From von Stutgardt's gun, or one of those Nazi Vultee pilots? Dave didn't know, and he didn't care. He put the bent disc to his lips and kissed it.

"And I said you were no luck charm?" he grunted. "Brother! I'm carrying you around for the duration. And I don't mean maybe!"

——THE END——
See next page.

A Page from

DAVE DAWSON WITH THE COMMANDOS

A FAINT SOUND broke the silence of the black night. Was it the wind in the trees? Was it a night animal stalking his next meal? Or was it one of Adolf Hitler's uniformed killers?

Dave didn't know. Perhaps it was just his imagination. Perhaps it was just his taut nerves snapping, and his brain playing him tricks. According to the report he had received he shouldn't run into any of the enemy for another twenty minutes at least. Just to make sure he pressed himself close to the ground, turned his cork-blackened face toward his left wrist, and with his right hand inched up the cuff of his sleeve so that he could see his radium dial wrist watch that circled his forearm halfway to the elbow.

Twenty minutes? His watch must be wrong! It must have gained two hours in the last ten minutes, for he was certain that it was only ten minutes ago when he had looked at it. Yet the watch said it was exactly five minutes of the hour. Twenty minutes? No, not twenty. There were only three minutes left! So that faint sound